ALMOST MIDNIGHT

ALMOST MIDNIGHT

BY DON BELTON

BTB
BEECH TREE BOOKS
WILLIAM MORROW
New York

Library of Congress Cataloging-in-Publication Data

Belton, Don.
Almost midnight.

I. Title.
PS3552.E5339A8   1986   813'.54   85-30753
ISBN 0-688-06342-X

Printed in the United States of America

First Edition

1 2 3 4 5 6 7 8 9 10

BOOK DESIGN BY LINEY LI

B⌐B

The word "book" is said to derive from *boka*, or beech.
The beech tree has been the patron tree of writers since ancient times and
represents the flowering of literature and knowledge.

For Charles Belton, Sr., Willie B. Wise,
Henderson Briggs and John Cornelius Coleman

. . . the time to favor her, . . . the set time, is come.
For thy servants take pleasure in her stones,
and favor the dust thereof.

ALMOST MIDNIGHT

1.

~~There~~ was singing in his dream. He had been at a river. The small, wrinkled women in summer dresses and field hats were sitting out on the rocks. He smelled magnolias and Spanish moss. He was transfixed staring up into green waving trees until the voice of the preacher called the children out into the water. He had on a white gown. The gown soaked up the river water and clung to his thighs. He was a little ahead of the other children. He waded through the water and mud as the women on the rocks sang in weary common meter "Run 'Long Mourner." He became buoyant in the water. The minister in the dream had a long, stiff, white beard. "Run your hand down my beard," said the preacher, "and the fear of Hell will leave you."

Daddy Poole was at the rear of 28 Prince Street on the second floor. Outside on the street the children were singing rhymes and leaping in the air. It was hotter here than a hundred degrees. In his room, in the shadows of potted plants, a slow light moved in a corner. The light moved over a painting of Christ with a crowned bleeding heart and eyes like cool muddy water. The painting of Jesus bulked big. The pierced heart in the chest. The liquid smile bearing the whisper: "Peace." The clock snickered on the nightstand. The plants mumbled. His hat and cane lay on a chair beside the bed. The time was almost ready.

The Venetian blinds were opened only a crack. Martha believed darkness kept the room cool. He barely breathed. The feeling of buoyancy returned from his dream.

Martha was in the kitchen next to his room cooking breakfast. The baby called Man played in the doorway between the two rooms. The smells from the kitchen admonished Poole. His hunger was not for what Martha was cooking.

His mother was in the room. Her breasts were heavy with milk though she was fifty years dead. As she approached him, her nipples hardened and forced at the hell-red cloth of her dress. At the bed she uncovered one of her breasts and guided it into the hungry old mouth of Daddy Poole. Her breast milk was cool and sweet. As he sucked, she disappeared.

Martha came into the room. Holding the baby, she lit a candle stub and stood by the blinds a moment. She came over by the bed and put Man on the floor. He crawled away, slapping the floorboards and laughing.

"Daddy, you done mess this bed? I just clean this goddamn bed. Don't you think I'm sick of cleaning shit? You worse than the goddamn baby." She jammed a cigarette in her fat mouth, lit it. "Well, roll on over."

She watched to see if he would move. He did not try to move. His eyes were glassy, fierce, staring up into her brow. Martha had heard him all night from her bed in the living room calling for people who were dead and laughing with them. Martha left the room and returned with a basin full of steaming water and rags. She wrenched her father to one side of the bed. He seemed to return to himself and called her name.

"Babygir'," he pushed the syllables from his mouth like water bubbles. "Babygir'?"

"Yeah," she answered him, "this Babygirl, Daddy. What you want?"

He looked worn-out and confounded. He had grown so frail and thin, it was hard to tell his body from the crumpled bed clothes.

"Babygirl," he said in the sustained tones of a very young man, "my testicles are cold."

Martha cleaned her father and changed the bed. She lit another cigarette. She leaned down and whispered in his ear. "Don't be afraid," she whispered.

He opened and shut one eye. He said, still sounding like another man, "Baby, your daddy aint hardly 'fraid." When he lifted his eye, his daughter and grandson were gone and more than half the day had passed.

He watched the light at the spaces in the blinds. The light was full of colors. It was as if someone had come and decorated his window with ribbons. The ribbons burned and danced around the room.

Martha had never been a child. She had not walked or spoken or played as a child. She played a woman's game and had played at being a woman as long as she could remember. She felt past being grown without ever becoming ripe. Men saw more in her than was there. Martha was maple-brown-skinned, with a round, flat face and regular features. Her eyebrows were shaved and represented with two heavy-handed pencil strokes. She was seventeen, and she looked twice her age. She had developed the physical characteristics of a woman in a cartoon: overlarge breasts and a tiny waist, and a generous behind and hips. Her arms were bulky, short and unwieldy. Martha looked incapable of running; she was sexual and perversely vulnerable.

Her hair was cut and processed every four weeks at Honey's on the Avenue. She would rather go without eating than have to miss her appointment at Honey's when money was scarce. She had not seen her baby's father for a year. His name was Ralston. He was a jet-black boy with a headful of sculptured curls. His nickname was Silk. One of Martha's girlfriends said he was living in North Newark with some other woman, studying to become a Muslim, calling himself Rasheed. Her girlfriend said he quit school like he always said he would, still did not have a job, but was playing the alto saxophone every Friday night at Mr. Wonderful's for no pay.

"I don't care what he's doing!" Martha snapped at Peanut, who claimed to know all about Silk's new life.

They were in Peanut's apartment, sitting on the sofa, sipping warm beer. Peanut did not own a refrigerator. Martha stopped there after work on Fridays before going to pick up Man from the baby-sitter's.

Peanut was a cocktail waitress at the Playbar.

"Shit," said Peanut, adjusting her wig at the nape of her head, "if my man ever got me pregnant and dropped out of sight for the best of a year and turned up living with some bitch 'cross town, I'd sure as hell care. I'd find him and kick his *and* his bitch's ass."

"You talking trash, Peanut, and you know it. You can't get pregnant no way. I aint got to go looking for Ralston. What do I want with Silk now? I aint like all these women that swear they can't live without some damn piece of man. And the way Archie kicks your behind over the least little thing, I wouldn't even talk such trash if I was you." Martha laid her beer can on the arm of the sofa. "Silk can stay where he is and do what he please. I'm worried about my father now," she said in a new voice. "That's all I'm worried about."

Peanut laughed. It was the same good laughter she usually saved for the hours right before dawn at the Playbar after she had been awake all night. "Girl," she said, holding her sides, "aint no need in letting his death tear you up. That's all your father's doing is dying. Maybe you aint realized even Jesus had to die, girl."

She looked at Martha, who received the look and held it awhile. Then Martha looked away.

Peanut laughed again, but when her smile wore off, there was nothing left in her face but a stare. The two girlfriends turned away from each other on the sofa. Martha got up and walked the length of the room. She looked as if she were turning something over in her mind.

Peanut wondered what her best sister was thinking. "You know something?" cried Peanut, drinking beer, getting foam on her chin. "You know one thing? Daddy got to be old as Methuselah by now. He might even be Methuselah. Daddy Poole lived a thousand lives in his time. He call you Babygirl because you supposed to be his last child, but before you he made so many sons and daughters don't nobody know the number. I know what I'm talking about. I been in Newark a long, long time."

Daddy Poole's last child sat down in a chair across the room and turned her back to her friend. Martha felt a sudden pressure in her sister's tone.

"You listen to Peanut, baby," she was saying, "listen to Peanut!"

Peanut was a skinny woman; she was forty-eight, and without makeup she looked bad for her age. She had a bad heart. Her doctor told her she had better be careful if she did not want to have a heart attack, but she drank at least three six-packs of beer a day, slept and ate little.

"Listen to Peanut: You got to let Daddy go! You get yourself a man and give your baby a father. Daddy need to be tired of living anyway. I hope to tell you, your father is the Devil. You don't know like I know. . . . "

Martha got furious. "I don't give a fuck what you think you know about my father, Peanut," she said significantly, turning to face the woman.

Peanut was in her underwear. She reached down and opened another beer. "Well, I'm going to tell it to you anyway—for free."

Martha got up and snatched her chair and carried it into the kitchen. The kitchen had a slop sink in it and every copy of the *Star Ledger* since 1947, neatly bound and stacked. Saving newspapers was Peanut's hobby.

The girl sat down in the windowless room. She couldn't stand for anybody to talk against her father. Not even Peanut. She had been friends with Peanut most of her life. In many ways Martha considered herself equal to Peanut. They were both clever women who had given themselves over to life. They struggled together and encouraged each other. Martha used to call Peanut Mom. After she had Man, she started calling her Peanut and Sister. Martha never knew another mother or sister. As soon as she was born, her real mother gave her to Daddy Poole and vanished.

Peanut called, "Come on out of that kitchen, girl. You think my voice can't carry in there?"

Martha let the water run in the sink.

"Turn off my water, fool."

"Go to hell."

Martha already knew all she wanted to know about her father. He said he came to Newark in 1927 with one suitcase. By the forties his picture appeared in newspapers and magazines above the caption: "Reverend 'Daddy' Poole, celebrated negro millionaire." She knew he had fathered sons and daughters everywhere. No one knew the number of his children, least of all Daddy. She knew he had children and women all over the world. He fathered Martha when he was in his eighties. By the time Martha learned to walk, he had already suffered his first stroke, was already retired from preaching. He lost his large church and the twenty-room house in Chatham, New Jersey. His followers rose and forced him from his pulpit in 1964. He packed his long car and drove back to Newark and closeted himself in 28 Prince Street. Gradually he began to rent portions of the house until finally he lived in the back of the second floor. He had rented the first floor to a shoeshine parlor for a while, but the parlor failed, and all that was left of the old shop was the storefront the bootblack had installed.

She knew about her father's churches, knew they had probably always been fronts for prostitution and the numbers game. She knew Daddy fucked his whores in Newark and overran the city with bastards. She was his daughter. He was fucking her when she was eleven. He had wanted to put her on the street, pulling ten-dollar tricks, but she ran away from him. She knew about her father.

"Come on back in here, Martha, and turn off my water. You aint paying my water bill. Get on in here," she said, irritable now. "Don't make me have to get off this couch."

Peanut heard the water go off. Martha came back in the room before long, her jaw set, her eyes swimming in tears.

"I hope you finished acting like a child." Peanut pursed her lips. "It's time you learned left from right, Miss. A lot of people don't like me because I talk too much. But it don't bother me. The truth is the truth and should be spoken at all times. I tell the truth, don't I? Peanut don't lie. I'm going to tell the truth till I drop dead. Your father aint shit. I know he aint shit. He know he aint shit. You know it too, but you done moved back in his house anyway. Taking care of him because he dying. Dying and aint got nobody. Shit. He need to die. I pray he can die." Peanut twisted around on the old couch trying to get comfortable. "How many niggers done died off the dope your father helped bring into these streets? How many young girls he done fucked and put on the street and left dried up and crawling with the rails?"

Martha started walking around the room. Her head hurt. She sipped air, felt her blood run warm for an instant. Her muscles were taut. "Shut up, Peanut. I don't want to hear this."

The barmaid bent her head to the side and looked over at the girl a little. "You going to listen, Martha. You got to look at what your father is, baby. You got to see his filth and—"

Martha's jaw began to shake. "Peanut, don't make me hurt you."

"—and give yourself a chance to be somebody. If he hadn't been so old when you was born, he woulda turned you out like all the rest, and you know it."

Martha whirled around and raised her hand to her friend.

Peanut reached for the long knife she kept hidden in the folds of the sofa. "Bitch," she said, "if you jump on me I'll cut you wide open."

Martha backed off. The barmaid shook the knife and went on talking. "He woulda turned you out like all the rest of us, selling your pussy. You can't count the colored women with scars from when Daddy Poole had his hooks in they backs. Now, you got to pack your things, girl, and get out his house. You got to do it now. Don't wait for him to die. Or he'll reach out and pull you down even in death. I know you balking because he was your father. But he wasn't just *your* father. He was everybody's father, and we all got to answer for the things he made us do."

Peanut waited before she put the knife away and said, "Get my leather skirt out the closet. I better start getting dressed for work. I don't even feel like moving today. What you think my new blouse would look like with my leather skirt?"

Martha did not answer her. She went to the closet and brought back a black glove-leather skirt and a red blouse. As she watched Peanut dress, she sucked her teeth and said, "Aint it kind of hot for leather?"

"It aint hot in the damn bar with that air-conditioner going."

"What shoes you going to wear?"

"My sling backs."

Martha tossed the shoes at Peanut's feet.

Peanut said, dragging a zipper up her side, "You know Silk is on that shit again, don't you?"

A light went on in Martha's eyes. She was headed for the closet again, singing something cool she'd heard on the radio. She turned to Sister and said, "I know he is."

It was almost evening. The children on Prince Street played, while upstairs at the back of 28, Daddy Poole lay dying in a bed that was now both deathbed and childbed. Across from 28, at 27 Prince Street, Sister Anderson sat on her porch with her two daughters, waiting. The children in the street played hide-and-seek, darting wildly, gasping and screaming. The child who was "it" hid her eyes against a post and cried:

> Two pounds of washing powder
> Two pounds of soap
> Who not ready holler: "billygoat"
>
> Apple, peach and pumpkin pie
> Who not ready holler: "I"

Sister Anderson rose from her sagging wicker chair and moved nervously by the screened windows on the porch. From the street she might have been mistaken for a shadow. The porch exterior was painted gray with a deep-green trim. The front yard—once an oasis of azaleas and rhododendrons—was now overgrown with elephant grass.

Her daughters sat at a miniature table on the porch solemnly handling a tea set. Patti, who was tall for her nine years, had on one of Sister Anderson's two-piece ensembles from the fifties, circular ear clasps and a gigantic picture hat with the veil pulled back, secured with a sapphire pin. The French high-heeled shoes almost fit her long feet.

Iphigenia had stuffed tissue paper in the backs of her mother's red pumps. The shoes were barely visible beneath the red cocktail dress draping the floor around the chair. The dress had a paper rose at the waist. She had balled up nylons and stuck them in the built-in brassiere. She wore a triple strand of pearls.

The crinoline under the cocktail dress made a whir each time Iphigenia moved in her chair. The girls whispered to each other. Patti complimented her sister on her hairstyle—a stately twist held with tiny mother-of-pearl combs.

In front of them, Sarah was monitoring the activity of the street children.

"Getting so now," she declared, running by the windows again, "you can't even sit on your porch without a lot of noise from other people's children."

Neither of her daughters acknowledged Sister Sarah's remark. They were accustomed to listening to her as one might listen to a singer singing in a new language. They never understood why she said what she did to them. Yet they could identify something like the ring of urgency or distress in her voice.

"Patti, dear, would you pass the toast, please," said Iphigenia, the oldest girl, referring to a piece of cardboard cut into the shape of a slice of bread. Her teeth were slightly bucked and she hated to open her mouth to speak.

"But, of course, precious Iphigenia," Patti replied softly, fussing with the hat a little. But her thin shoulders tightened as she braced herself for her mother to go on, as she had every afternoon that summer, about the noise the other children made on the street.

"It's getting to be too much for me. I just can't stand it," said Sister Anderson, tracing her steps back to her chair. She applied her hands to her heart and massaged her breasts. "I'm moving off this street full of niggers!"

Move then, thought Iphigenia. *Rent a truck and move.* Their mother had money locked up and hidden all over the house, and she was always crying poor.

Patti wished her mother would go in the house and shut her mouth before some of the neighbors heard what she was saying. It was bad enough she and Iphigenia were not allowed to play with any of the children on the block. "Better not see you playing with them niggers!" their mother was always telling them. "Better stop popping your fingers and prancing around to music like niggers. This is a home, not a barrelhouse!"

Patti and Iphigenia lived in number 27 with their mother and father. They never played with the children from the neighborhood. Because their father was away so much of the time, driving a long-distance hauler for a supermarket chain, they lived mostly with their mother in the three-and-a-half-story house with the screened porch. All their father did was go to work and come back home, go and come back. It was a wonder if he knew Patti and Iphigenia apart.

The girls were allowed no contact with their neighbors except an occasional, reserved *hello,* a quiet *good morning,* a gracious *good evening.* These were the ways their mother had taught them. These ways, they were taught, were to show the mean pack of niggers, who stayed on Prince Street, that they were not howlers or runners of the street, but were as pure and pacific as little white girls. As imperial as the white girls they observed in school or met in their storybooks.

Everyone said they were such nice colored girls, even if Sister Anderson had no business having them so late in life. They were only a year apart in age. Their mother dressed them in matching outfits like twins. They even wore matching shoes. They had beige faces and impudent brown eyes. Their beauty was easy to see. They had long reddish hair that was almost straight, almost supple, like their mother's. They knew they were rare and not "common." They were not ordinary children, their mother said.

The Andersons had lived on Prince Street longer than any of their present neighbors except Daddy Poole. Sam Poole lived there back when the Germans and Irish did not want even the Jews to move in. It was still a clean neighborhood when Sarah and her husband moved there during the forties and proudly began to pay the mortgage on 27, almost thankful to be among the few negroes on the block. Sister Anderson had shopped along Springfield Avenue and Broadway for perfect objects to fill the house. She had the house painted gray and green. She had screened in the front porch, though the street was quiet. The trees were healthier then; altogether different spirits lived inside them. The breezes in seasonable weather talked, and the rubbing leaves and branches whispered. That was before the "fat Jews," who by then ruled Prince Street, packed up and made their exodus to Vailsburg, the Oranges and Montclair.

The windows on Prince Street had been beacons of order and contentment. Life was worth everything it cost. That was before the janitors, maids and nurses over on High Street vanished. Before the number 9 bus was rerouted to drive back and forth all day and night through Prince Street. Before the cutters and rapists and snatchers "jumped so bad" that lurid bright lights were installed above the maple trees. Before the maple trees began to yellow even in summer.

But the mortgage payments continued, and meaner-looking immigrants from the black South came and filled the neighborhood with their particular baggage. And now those children—those other people's children—made all that noise on Prince Street. To Sarah, it was the sound of a hundred flies playing in the sores of a dead thing. The windows of the houses, no longer beacons, emitted, when she searched them from her porch at night, a visible darkness. They were windows to rooms where life, like a light, had gone out.

Sarah went on talking from her chair. "When I moved into this house, I felt like I was finally receiving my portion of God's promise. I felt like old Lot; I wasn't about to look back at the burning past. But I was looking in a mirror made for fools. If I could have looked into the future and seen *this* day, I would have stayed in Jefferson County, Georgia.

"But, no, I had to have my Newark. I used to love this old town like I was loving a person. But it was different times and different people. But, Lord, if I could have looked and seen this day. . . . The white folks just flew out of here. I can't blame them. Lord knows I wished I could move someplace. I could have moved too. But your father said he was already working two jobs and overtime. I was willing to work, but he wouldn't have it. I was willing to follow the dream as far as needed. I was willing to go all the way. But your father . . . He would only buy sweepstakes tickets and buy chances and talk about how a gypsy woman told him he was going to come into a great sum of money. Telling me how when his ships came in he was going to take all that big money and move me to a place four times as nice as Newark. Well, you see I'm still right here on this porch, don't you? I reckon I'll be right here when I die."

Sarah Anderson played fretfully with her fingers. Her daughters watched her, certain she was about to have one of her fits.

Sarah stood up and straightened her dress. She was staring across the street at Daddy Poole's house, listening to the echoes of her memories.

"Well, at least Daddy didn't move," she addressed the porch. "He stayed on, just like us. I guess, before long he'll be gone too. Gone on. To his reward. That man was a blessing to this entire neighborhood. Daddy Poole was a blessing to the world. Was a time didn't a summer pass he didn't take all the neigh-

borhood kids to the shore for an outing. In the winter he had
such parties in that house. And he drove some long cars in his
day. And sported those young women he called his ponies. Poor
Daddy Poole, somewhere in that house, dying and got to listen
to those terrible children making all that noise."

2.

"A woman's only human . . .
you should understand . . ."
—Song

~~~ She watched Martha return, stiff-backed, with a red
silk scarf in her hand, from the closet. Her eyes went over the
girl slowly, as if Martha's truncated form contained some new
mystery. Martha was old past her years, generations and wars
older than the perilous seventeen years she called a girlhood. It
was frightening and fascinating to see: Martha possessed the
hard, river-cold eyes of a survivor. Her full, heavy bosom
seemed to define comfort. Her small, square hands were already
ruined by work and worry; the shoulders already hunched over
with three centuries of burden-bearing and blind hoping for a
way out of no way. Too many women—too many mothers, sisters, sweethearts and fire-hot bitches lived inside that girl—
walked with her in a troubled, mutual rhythm. It was as though
the true child named Martha Renée Poole had been robbed from
the crib by ghosts and replaced by this: an impostor, a demonic
commonwealth of lost souls.

"You know," said Peanut, seating herself importantly on the

sofa again, "anybody could easy blame your father for what's happening to Silk and the rest of these junkies in Newark. Your big-time father helped bring that poison into these streets. First it was running his whores. Then the numbers racket. During World War Two it was *him* the white gangsters used to start selling that shit—Big H, horse, stuff—to the niggers in Newark. His churches been the cover for some of *everything*. Before that shit come over here from the East, we aint hardly knowed nothing about it. Niggers was satisfied with they gin and reefers. Them boys what was serving in C.B.I.—that was China, Burma, India—they was the ones started first getting messed up with the opium drugs. They came back here, when Uncle Sam was through with them, like a troop of walking deads. Soon they little brothers and the girls was using it too. I seen a fellow on that mess walk right into a moving car without blinking an eye. The thing about that horse, that heroin, is that it straightens you out. Liquor will fuck you up, but the Big H, baby, before long you be taking it to get straight—just to feel like a human being. Back in the forties, when that shit hit the streets good, women was knifing they men to get it. Them old joy bangers would sell they own mama to cop a fix. The little boys was holding up mom-and-pop stores to get money to buy it.

"Was a time right here in this city when you didn't have to lock your door at night. When it was real hot in the summer the people would take a blanket and go out and sleep in the park. Aint nobody even think of messing with them, but ever since the heroin come to town, we been living in our last days."

Martha was stopped in the middle of the faintly patterned floor, standing in a cage of light. She jerked the silk scarf and made it dance angrily at her right hip. Martha said, "Sister, how come you always got be going over and over them dead times? You always steady running your mouth about a lot of shit I don't know or care nothing about. You better go to work before your ass is fired."

"Longhead Pete won't fire me. Since he been making good money and hired them young barmaids, I don't do that much no how except sit up in there. Shit, he keep me because Peanut *is* the Playbar—at least to the rough crowd what come there, and Pete know it," she said fast. Then, as though suddenly hearing Martha's question for the first time, she shouted, "Because somebody's got to tell it. Because it's got to be told!" She stood and met Martha in the middle of the floor. Her voice became a soft summer sound. "Them times aint dead. They real." Here she pressed two fingers inside the palm of Martha's right hand. Martha felt the touch after the fingers were removed. "Time is time, girl. Them is the days what *made* today and made every day to come."

For a moment the hardness of Martha's body gave way to a grudging reverence for Peanut. Her body slackened under the pressure of marveling at the wisdom that often cut, like jagged lightning, through Peanut's plain, proud words.

Peanut put her face close to Martha's and stared into the old eyes inside the young girl's face. "God knows," she cried, "I don't believe in living in the past. This aint even about the past really. It's about all the stories of the women what lived it—and seen—coming together into one story. I'm drumming it into you same as my mother drummed it into me. The biggest problem with niggers is they don't know they own history. And you got to know your history, else you just going up against a beast, baby, like Little David without a sling."

She pulled back, returning to her sofa, her eyes drawn to gleaming slits. Her gaze was closed, like she had understood at last the mystery Martha held. She sank into the sofa. Her face fell back in a shadow. A large fly grazed her brow, sailing to the screen inside the window. Peanut took no notice of it.

Martha saw something dark form behind Peanut's eyes.

"Look, girl, just go on and live your life!" The words were cast out into the room like jangling coins. "You got to do it how you feel it. I *am* all the time talking to you like you part of something started long before you was born. But you *are* a part of it. You the last link on the chain of your father's women. You the link what could break and set us all free."

Martha could not say anything.

"You been here before. You always been as much woman as me. You got the old mother wit. You was a smart child—like a spirit what lived before. I see a whole lot more woman in you than you look like now, girl, strapped down with Silk's baby and cleaning the shit off Daddy's ass. That man shoulda *been* in a state home."

Martha sprang forward, her fixed face refracting light and shadow. "How do you see me, Sister?" she said hotly. "You always talking around it—about how I ought to be this thing or the other thing and what my father aint. But why don't you just break it down for me. How you see me?"

This question went unanswered for a long time. It hung there in the room, suspended above their heads. Before the shadows and dust could absorb the question completely, Peanut brushed aside a forelock of fake dead-black hair and said, "I see you walking, baby—clean and free. Walking for yourself and for all the women come before you. Women what could have walked. Free women what couldn't *claim* they freedom, that's all. I'm talking about some good women, Martha—your daddy's whores and women—women what could have walked free but it wasn't *in time* for them to have no freedom or peace. I'm going to tell you just what I mean."

"Talk on it," Martha said with a challenge in her voice, and sat in the chair opposite the sofa.

The room was steamy hot. Peanut looked greasy and messy. "First," she said, "go on in my bedroom and bring me my makeup case."

Martha pushed aside four empty beer cans and placed the opened makeup case in front of Peanut on the coffee table. Peanut smeared the beige liquid foundation over her face and neck. Then she dotted under her eyes, the center of her chin and nose with the cover stick. "A whole lot of women been messed up with your father. Not only colored women, but white ones too, all kinds. Not just here in Newark, but all over. One thing about all of them: Once Daddy marked them, they never got free. That include me."

She took the makeup brush and dusted her face with powder, staring at the mirror inside the case, crouching forward. "That include Sarah Anderson with her high-tone self sliding back and forth now every Sunday to the Pentecostal Church. You can look in that woman's face and tell she aint free in her mind. Once Daddy Poole put his hook in a woman back, she been his to meet in Hell for eternity. I know it to be a fact."

Martha was standing over the sofa. She wrapped the red silk scarf around her left hand and made a fist. "My mother—whoever the hell she was—she got away. Sure as hell, she walked free."

Peanut stretched her gross lips and smeared them with frosted lipstick. Her mouth resembled a glazed doughnut. "*That's* another dream you need to wake up from, girl! I don't care what lies your father told you about how your mother disappeared from around here."

"Dream my ass," she said. "It aint no fucking dream the way she walked out on me and my father before I could get a good look at her. I wonder do I ever cross that woman's mind. When I was little, I used to always be thinking she might come back for me. Even if she didn't take me nowhere, maybe she might come back for a little while and just hold me. I used to think I might see her anywhere—any strange woman I might see walking on the street could be her. I used to think like that and wonder what there might be in me or about me that she might recognize, so that she would know—on sight—that I was Martha; I was her child. Then I growed up. I got hip and had a baby my own damn self. Yeah, I mighta had no business having a baby at sixteen. Aint had no business doing what I was doing with Silk. Shit, I was doing my thing. But I know God forgive me cause at least I aint had no abortion, and least I aint run off and leave my baby like my dog of a mama did."

The words seemed to cut Peanut.

She said solemnly, closing the lid on the makeup case, "Baby, you need to hush," with a tenderness Martha could feel inside her chest. "Your mother is dead, child."

Martha looked at Peanut as if she were trying to figure out who she was or where they were. She stared at Peanut in that awful cornucopia-shaped wig with its supernumerary waves and curls. The face under the wig looked as though it were smeared with ashes.

She could only whisper, "You know about my mother, Sister?"

Peanut proffered her face. "All this time—I aint said a word. It's the part I just never felt strong enough or evil enough to tell. But now the time is too close. It's too close. Your father is going out, baby. Here it is Friday. He going to quit it—you and I both know it—before another Friday. Didn't you tell me you heard him last night talking to the spirits? It's time for the whole story to be told.

"Your Daddy got to pay for the shit he dealt women. That's how come you need to leave his house—now. Leave him up in there in that old house by hisself for the Devil to get him—to come and rip his soul out the core of his heart and drag him down time eternal. Wouldn't nobody else go up there even to look on him—not after what he done. Listen to me," she said, seductive as a virgin about to undress for her husband. Peanut opened another beer. "I'm going to tell you something to remember."

She's dead to the world, thought Iphigenia, pretending to sip from the plastic toy cup. She smoothed the lap of the shimmery-shiny cocktail dress and gave Patti the agreed-upon sign. She stood and walked to the sagging wicker chair where her mother was slumped like a drug-user, her eyes shattered by some hallucination, muttering to herself.

The tiny crystals hanging on Iphigenia's ears spun like distant planets as she stole up on her mother behind the big chair.

The phone started ringing inside the house.

Patti held her floppy hat, running to the vestibule door, trying not to laugh all over herself.

This was their game—Patti's and Iphigenia's—when *she* was having one of her spells—if they felt strong enough or evil enough. It was easy to hide on the porch—behind the fanback chair, in the doorways, in a long shadow. The first time they hid from her, when the summer started, they were amazed by their total invisibility. They could look right at her, and she would not see them. It was as though her eyes were looking at two places at the same time, one on top of the other. Once she peed her housedress, she was so outside herself, until her daughters' shocked laughter brought her back—back from wherever it was the ghosts took her mind. That was what Savannah, the grandmother with her good leg missing and the other one always full of cold and arthritis, said. *Dead to the world.* The grandmother said ghosts were making a fool of Iphigenia's mother. Ghosts were making her do everything but pray for her soul.

Iphigenia could not do a thing but watch.

Every time the phone rang something in her jerked to cold and complete attention. Since '64, or was it '65? The old times had been dead. Hairstyles were big and natural. The music was different—polyrhythmic, loud, jarring, but soulful the way it had been when she was young. But in '64 or '65, she was not young anymore.

Newark had gone a winter and a spring without him. He came back from France—Montmartre—and disappeared in his house. He did not say a word to anyone. The girl, his latest "new one" (she was his last one) was living with him in 28. After her he would have some old woman up there from time to time, buying liquor, cigars and Slim Jims off her government check. But the girl he brought back in '64 or '65 was the last: cooled-down and sweet café-au-lait skin, startled doe eyes, long rich-grade hair. The last of Daddy's legendary women.

He came back whenever it was—twenty years ago soon—and did not say a word.

"You were a good man, Sam Poole," Sarah called out from her chair. "A *great* man, but you were selfish."

Her eyes stared across the street at number 28 as if she could already see his spirit roiling up like smoke, leaving the house, Newark and leaving the world.

Iphigenia moved along the rear wall in a whir of crinoline and touched her sister at the door. Patti gave a devilish, gap-toothed smile. She fell on her knees and crawled up behind the fanback chair, with her shoes in her hands.

"Yes, you were good," she said, talking like some worn out church mother witnessing at Wednesday night prayer service. "But you were selfish—a selfish god in man. One thing I could never understand is why you wouldn't let no one love you good as you loved yourself."

The phone rang as Sarah talked over it.

"Here it has been since before the riot . . . I been waiting for you to just pick up your phone and call and say . . . Jesus only knows what . . . that you still remember the old times and still have some of the old love for your children."

Why in the world she never picked up her phone to call him never entered her mind. All these years, still waiting, even though nine years ago she sat on the same porch in the same fanback chair and watched the telephone men come and go in a truck and take every phone out of number 28. She was still waiting for that call. All these years—almost twenty soon—and she couldn't stand for herself or anyone else to stay on the phone longer than necessary.

Daddy might be trying to get through.

Patti was the first to creep around to the front of the chair and look in her mother's face.

Sister Sarah's eyes were a filmy gray. "Plenty of phones," she declared. "I never seen anybody keep so many phones in a house—different lines and all different colors with the wires to match. He had six phones if he had one. How many times did I sit up there with him in his sunroom when it was his office, him at his long oak desk talking on a red phone, a black phone, a white phone, when he was getting ready for one of his preaching tours? I sat and watched him make a million dollars one day over the phone. He loved to get down to business, talking all afternoon in his grave voice till his shoulders and arms were tight, drinking a hundred cups of coffee and mouthing cigar stubs. Moochie, Red Bobby and Mr. Henderson, the fellows from the church closest to Daddy, would come in at the end of the day. Moochie would start right off telling Daddy jokes in a mild voice. Red Bobby would walk Daddy over to a leather-covered table and massage him with linseed oil and camphor. Mr. Henderson read Daddy all the sports scores and anything else out the *Star Ledger* he thought he might like. I'd be right up there, smoking my Benson and Hedges and listening to jazz on the radio. Sometimes I'd massage Daddy's feet. He liked for me to massage his feet.

"Sometimes, on those evenings, after Red Bobby was through massaging him, if Mrs. Lyons didn't already have dinner laid out downstairs in the dining room, and he wasn't in a hurry to bathe and dress, he would lay up on that leather table, with a towel wrapped around his middle like a huge baby, and just talk—over the radio and all the evening sounds on Prince Street. He would only be talking about life, the nature of people, of things, but those soft evening talks by Daddy up in that room would be like seminars of the magnitude that people travel day and night and pay money to attend.

"*Who* you been in there talking to these years you haven't even shown your face to nobody that loves you but that poor, half-crazy Martha? Even when the child had to take you back and forth to the hospital, you had some old muslin over your head like a dead man and her standing guard over you with a stick. Wild, half-crazy girl and wouldn't nobody dare try her and that stick. Lord knows it wasn't girl or stick, but you and your magic that's kept us all at bay. When you going to let us close around you again? When you're dead and finished? When you going to touch us and heal us and bless us one more time?

"I know you sent that riot—conjured it like God calls up a fire in the wilderness. Folks said it was the Muslims that instigated it, or some other militants, or the police themselves just for an excuse to whip negro heads, but it was *you*. The burning streets and burned-out, gutted-out stores and houses, mothers and babies shot up on their own porches—called it up as a judgment on Newark. You let the last life-air be sucked on out of this city—retribution for how we failed you all those years ago when you closed down your churches and gave your last sermon. Went away and left us. Then came back with that girl—your last whore—and dared a man to knock on your door. Nobody dared, knowing you, knowing and not knowing what awful thing you might have waiting inside. So those who had known you and loved you and lifted you up, seen the miracles you worked right here in these streets, tried to forget you, left you alone.

"What you wanted with that last whore I knew and everybody knew without needing you to say a word. You wanted her to give you a son that was yours. The way my Emmett was for you before my mother took him away. She did it. Now he's grown. I barely got to raise him. *I* lost him myself. Grown and don't half-write his own mother to see if she in this world or the next. But that French-bred nigger, that strong-backed bitch tricked you and gave you Martha, a flat-nosed, nappy-headed woman-child. Where she went after that I don't know, and I don't care. Was a time an army of women would have given their soul to bear you a son. And an army of women did. But with all those sons, Sam, you wanted mine, my Emmett. You used to play with him, look at him lying in his crib and say, 'What are you: angel or child, black or white, boy or girl?' That was one beautiful child. He was a *beautiful* baby. But once you started taking him around—once you filled him with your dream—Mama, *she* took him away from you. She was scared you would do all with him what you did with me, but Emmett was a boy. I tried to tell Mama. She said I was crazy. But I just trusted you. He was only five years old. I wasn't a baby, I went with you out of my own free will, and I was doing everything I was grown enough to do. If I went with those white men for you, that was my business. Long as you were my man, and you were still laying down with me. . . ."

The telephone rang for the thirteenth time and stopped. Only Savannah Sparks, the grandmother, would ring the phone like that. Iphigenia rushed to the chair as her mother cried fiercely:

"I don't care about none of it. I just love *you*, that's all!"

Laughter spilled from Patti's mouth.

"I just want you to look on me and speak my name. All I want to know is that I have your forgiveness. This whole city—the people and the houses—is drying up needing your glance. A glance isn't too much to ask, is it? We all loved you. Even the stones in the streets loved you when you led your parades down Springfield Avenue. Please, Daddy. Come on out that house!"

The girls scrambled to get out of the way as Sister Sarah leaped from the chair, arms outstretched, and fell like a ruined effigy on the floor. The girls narrowed their eyes and compressed their lips, staring down on their mother, compassionless as spies.

Suddenly, her eyes awakened. She felt her way back to the chair with a humiliated look on her face, looking at her daughters look at her.

"What you looking at me like that for? Stop it, you hear me?"

"Can't nobody look at you?" Patti asked in a sassy singsong.

Iphigenia started to speak but repented. She pushed her top lip tight over her bucked teeth and whirled around.

"Where you going, daughter?" Sarah asked.

"To play with my new doll," Iphigenia answered over her shoulder, in motion toward the vestibule door. "I got to do her hair. She's French and just as mean and black as those streets."

Patti turned quickly following her sister.

"And where you going?"

"To call public service on my play phone. They been worrying me about a bill."

The children trotted off into the house.

Sarah sat on the porch putting her mind in order. The telephone rang. This time, on the second ring, she stood and went into the house, returning after a moment, talking on the cordless phone.

"Well Mama," she was saying—"I only heard it ring just now. It's a wonder I can hear anything with these wild children ripping and running in the street"—going by the screened porch windows. "Maybe you dialed wrong. Are you wearing your glasses?"

"Don't ask me about those damn glasses," the serpent-soft voice came crackling into Sarah's ear. "I threw them out with the trash last Tuesday. I told that fool optometrist, when he had me buy them in the first place, I don't need glasses. I can see more than I want to see. Seen enough if I go stone-blind this same evening. I didn't dial your number wrong either . . . long as I been dialing your damn number!"

Savannah Sparks drew a long breath and sent it over the wire. "Now, what in the world is the matter, you haven't called me all day? Those girls all right?"

"They're fine. Nothing's the matter. I've just been sitting," she said, falling back in her chair, "sitting on this porch and studying."

"Studying about what? I know you're staring at his house. Anything going on over there?"

"What's going to go on?"

"You know as well as I do that man is dying. I dreamed his death three nights running. I've *known* death by its calling signs since I was Patti's and Iphigenia's age. I've seen it too many times—came and took my mother and father out of this world walking the wind. Daddy is going to die."

"I dreamed it myself," Sarah said, afraid, "this morning sitting on this porch. I fell asleep while the girls were playing in the back. Seemed to me I was passing on a street full of snapping crocodiles. The streets were so treacherous with crocodiles I had to make my way along the porches of the row houses till I came to the house he was in—Daddy's house. Long, empty, blinding-bright rooms and, in the middle of it, a stairway turning—looked like forever—on top of itself. He came out the back of the house from around the stairs with that big old Stetson hanging on the side of his head—you know how he would wear it—shading his left eye. He was dressed back: boxy iridescent suit, black patent-leather pumps, long cape, rings on all his fingers. Came right up to me where I was standing and pressed my hand hard. I was looking dead in his mouth at those gold-tipped teeth shining like a row of suns all risen up at the same time in the sky.

"'If you don't mind,' he said, 'I believe I'll go upstairs awhile.' Kissed me lighter than a baby's kiss and moved on up the stairs, breaking down and disappearing, getting older with every step . . .'"

"That was it. God is a time-god, honey, and He's killing every one of us by the time," said Savannah. "His daughter come home yet?"

The two women were silent for a while over the phones.

"No, ma'am. She is due to pass here directly, I guess, coming home from work with that baby—that *Man*—on her hip."

"Could be up there dead right now. I ought to call the emergency wagon myself."

"No, Mama, stay out of it. He doesn't want us in it."

"Hell, what do I care? I stayed out of it this long. Go ahead, Daddy, and die your death. I heard his first sermon in Newark and I heard his last. I remember when he used to set up tents in the empty lots and preach. He broke those crutches, and the people would go off walking and praising God. One thing I'll say for him, he could preach awhile, couldn't he? Preached that he would never die. Over the radio. Stunned my soul: 'I am going to *run* . . .'"—Savannah's voice had turned into a pounding basso shower—"'Run and not faint. I am going to *fly* . . . and never falter. I will renew my strength again . . . and again. I will rise up and heal this city. I will show my prowess generation after generation.' Remember how he would preach it, child?"

"Lord, yes," Sarah said. "Daddy could talk his talk. The way that man could hit on a phrase and bust it wide open. . . . He could make anything true. That was his power. He preached that all through the thirties—that he wouldn't die, he was God, and didn't the people believe in him—the poor as well as the rich? Then he changed over during the war, starting calling himself God's ambassador, and didn't miss a beat. His followers missed not a beat either. 'I am . . .'—grumbling like a dry thunder—'the Ambassador to the King of Heaven.'"

Savannah's giant laugh came clear and bright from her apartment on Hillside Place. "One thing Daddy showed was just how foolish people are. How in the world he going to be God Himself, and then God's ambassador and doing his business like any other man with a wildness dangling in between his legs."

"I still won't set myself up to judge against Sam Poole."

"You know as well as me he was wicked and corrupt."

"All I know is what he did for me. He never showed me anything but a dignified gentleman with a Big Daddy heart with room for *everybody*. All I know is the wonders he did—not only in Newark but in Europe, Africa, Japan and South America. I saw what he meant to people. What other man do you know—with a drop of negro blood—to rise up and be the king Daddy was for people—rise up out of these streets? I won't let anyone talk him down before me. Whatever he was, he was a good man, an *old* spirit. I went off with him when I was twenty and he was sixty-two. He showed me things as a young woman that Hindus and other people walk over coals and starve themselves to learn. We had our little fights. Finally we broke off. Look like nothing between us now except dust and distance, but I still ask about him when I see his last child going and coming from his house. I feel sorry for that child; I think she believes it about her father that he's God and won't die."

"He just filled that girl's head with nonsense since she was old enough to listen and too young to understand."

"The way she has had him before every doctor in this city, all the evangelists, spiritualists and Cassandras she has ushered back and forth through that house—when he forbade any of us who knew him to ever cross the door . . ."

"I don't know where she gets the money—those doctors and things cost money's mammy."

"She gets it scrubbing floors for those Italians out in Belleville every day but the day her social worker comes around so she won't lose her little welfare check. She don't look like she half eats. I give her something every once in a while and make her buy food for that mannish baby. I know I shouldn't do it. Jimmy Anderson would throw a fit if he knew I do it. I believe

37

it, though; she really thinks he won't die. That's why she's wearing herself out. I believe that child is waiting for her father to laugh at death."

"Sam Poole has got to be a hundred years old. He's *got* to die. Death is the debt we all must pay. That son of a bitch can't go on fooling with God forever."

Sarah's voice was tired. "Well, let me hang up this phone and get in the house. I have to get dinner."

"You don't have to get it now. Those girls are used to eating at eight o'clock and Jimmy's on swing shift and won't be home till midnight. It bothered you what I just said about Sam, didn't it? You still believe in him, don't you?"

"I left Sam Poole's church in 1956! I haven't *seen* him since those few years before the riot."

"I didn't ask you any of that!"

In a cold, hoarse whisper Sarah gave up her confession: "I'm just holding on—and I can't let go of my faith."

3.

*"Daddy loved women,
but he hated womenkind."*
—WILLA MAC EARLE (PEANUT)

〰〰 "I'm going to tell you how it was with your mother in them early sixties, before you opened your eyes to the world." Martha's mind drowned in that voice—a liquid, slow voice spelling out the story: "How it was for all us black sisters scuffling in these streets. Your father had his churches some of every place: Newark, Harlem, Detroit, Philly, Chicago. Plus big overseas missions. But I'm talking about Newark to you. If all the rotting houses on this hill could talk they couldn't tell half the story I can.

"I'm going to tell you exactly where it's at, so there won't be no place left to hide." She shook her head and slapped her hands together. "Peanut is where it's at, and I don't lie for nobody.

"The time came when every white person and every black person with more than two nickels to rub together had moved clean off this hill—clean out of Newark. The black ones following jobs and the chance to live as close as they could to the white ones, like dingy smudges at the borders of something white and clean. The white ones was busting loose in places like Short Hills and Scotch Plains with the money they worked hard for and they parents worked hard for here in Newark. Money they was still grinding out in them offices downtown and in the stores on Springfield Avenue. They still own these dried-out rickety houses we got to fight with rats to live in. White men was using this hill for a toilet—just like they daddies used it before I was born—and using the colored woman for a mat to wipe they feet on. In that day, the colored woman was too black to get hired for a decent job, but she wasn't too black for one of them to go to bed with on a Friday night.

"In them fierce, raging days (before Newark exploded and the riot in '67 set the streets on fire) a black woman couldn't walk the streets at night without some car slowing at every corner, full of white men or good-timing Montclair negroes taking her for a whore. I was turning my tricks and carrying my butcher knife in my handbag, because even the working girls had to watch out or else a gang of men might jump her and take her pussy and leave her, legs up, in some alleyway, mumbling to herself. Worst thing can happen to a whore is the gang-up. You don't never live it down. What to speak of some mother coming home from working in a factory all night, trying to get in her door before her children wake up—*if* she can get her ass through a war zone.

"That was the Newark you fell out into, screaming into hell's black hole: but into a world of black girls not made of trouble alone. This hill is where we been pressing on and getting up and making ways out of no way—back from the day you wasn't allowed to do nothing but scrub a lady's toilet or be some man's whore. I aint never been a lady, and I sure aint no man. I know I been through enough shit to make a garden of good flowers.

"Back then, I wasn't like I am now. I was young. I loved to fight. I wasn't necessarily looking for any particular person to fight. I was fighting with the trouble my soul was in. I always been a very short-nerve person. I would cut in a minute anybody who worked my last nerve. My patience ran thinner than it does today. I was always saying something I didn't mean and talking loud in somebody's face. I laugh loud now, but when I was young, I was loud, period. One time a bitch pulled a gun on me, talking about I was trying to steal her man. I got up in front of the bitch's gun and cussed her to her teeth. 'Yeah baby, I will steal your man.' Then I beat her ass with her bad gun from the juke-joint entrance to the parking lot.

"Fighting and running the streets: That was my meat. I ran with a crowd. My crowd was bar whores and faggots. The faggots was effeminate, but they was big. They could dress up in all the women's clothes they please and stick fake hair under they long veils and be scratching up them bar floors with high heels and pricking the air with perfume—but them faggots could all fight and would throw down in a minute. The bars was wild, and in that day, the Hill was a wide-open district. Almost every corner had a bar and every bar had a back room. Them rough-party negroes raised the devil every day on this hill from midnight to noon, but they pitched a real mess on Friday night. Some places bust out with they shit on Saturday night, but up here the night was Friday. That was the night all the rackets had they payday. Your daddy paid everybody on Friday. His workers got they money on Friday. He paid his women on Friday too.

"Some of everything would go on in them bars—fighting, cutting—and I seen some of all of it. I've had poison put in my drink twice. Still I loved to run the streets. It wasn't just me; the times was on a hard boil. I could deal with it too. All you young kids what came after my generation, you think you be into something with your little clubs and jumping music, but the jam is dead. It's just barely moving, but it's dead. There won't never be nothing again like when your father was running the

Hill with his women. One thing I'll say for Daddy, he made the whole city swing.

"I started running in these streets when I was eleven years old, and I was still running them in 1962—when the heavy change came. My mother knew I was wild. She tried to tell me. 'Daughter,' she would say, 'there aint a thing in them streets.' I think about my mother sometime, her crooked neck and twisted spine, and how *she* paid for her young wildness, but then I felt like saying, 'Woman, go to hell.' She was right. Aint nothing in the streets. I'm still learning that very thing old as I am and still running them. I just slowed down, that's all.

"Back in '62 I was turning my tricks and running with my crowd, but my mother never found out I was a prostitute. That's how come I thank God for one thing: that with all my mother suffered and all the things what crucified that woman, at least I wasn't kicking more nails in her every time I threw open my thighs for some john. She died two years before I pulled down my first ten dollars for laying out a man.

"In 1962 the dope and the syphilis was eating the guts out of this hill. We was stealing from each other, killing each other. Offing ourself. Offing our own. I remember when negroes used to make a joke that suicide was for rich white people. Through the slavery time and night riders down South, through Depression and wars, negroes kept on striving and bouncing back like prize fighters. Now it looked like we'd finally come to erasing ourself by our own hand—with that dope and the things it will make you do, with a packet of powder no bigger than a dose of Stanback. In '62 we was one big suicide pact. Most of the negroes couldn't even say it right—*harry-on* and *hey-roan*—so they made up all the nicknames: 'smack,' 'H' for short and 'boy.' That shit had been in this city's blood for twenty years. Police wasn't doing a damn thing about it. The mob boys was cleaning up on this hill, selling it right in the playgrounds. Why shouldn't they? They kids was safe in the suburbs.

"Your daddy was sweating it out in France.

"That was the year I started going with Jake. Jake Means was a lieutenant in your father's church. He was a man what really loved God, but he loved whiskey just a little bit better. He used to hang out in the bar I tricked out of that winter—over on West Kinney Street. He wouldn't mess around with none of the other liquor heads or the bar girls. He would sit up to the bar and have his drinks. He'd play the jukebox though, and that's how I got to tell he could dig a pretty good groove. One night I asked him to punch A-Seven—that was my song: 'You Don't Know What It Means.' Jackie Wilson could sing that thing. We slow-dragged out in the middle of the little bar floor. I could smell his nervousness. I could feel his curved up prick growing hard and real against my belly. I think I fell in love with that boy behind that one dance. He was different. He wasn't all rough. He was holding me like I was a jewel he'd found. I *was* a young, sweet, slim thing then. I had long, processed hair. I had some righteous hair. I had the prettiest white teeth. My face, my arms, my legs was red and shining like pomegranates. Now my hair under this old wig done broke off and turning white. My teeth is falling out of my head one by one. But then I was a well-put-together something. I was a real jitterdoll. I was giving up all the woman I was, at that moment, in my dance. I was dancing out my soul, getting down into his mind, getting all down into his heart.

"Jake was a square, but he knew what I was. He had it in his mind to make a decent woman out of me. I'd already planned to square up before I met Jake anyway. It was only a matter of time. I knew I'd had it, and I was just waiting to make my move. Most whores never get enough of running down that game. I knew I was different. I didn't have a pimp by then and wasn't looking for one. If a john tried to kick my ass and take my money, I could go for myself.

"That night me and him got a little thing going, and I played along like he was saving me. Shit, I wasn't no fool. That kid (I say kid because that's all either one of us was then, though Jake was seven years older than me) was *built* from the ground up. He had a dick long as a quart of liquor and almost as good. You could tell he had a fine dick by the way he sat and walked. He had real light eyes that looked green but was gray. I never had a man love me better or treat me with more respect than Jake. Jake Means gave me the love what made me, what I'm *still* made of today. All the men I've had coming down the years, filling me with they hard, nasty love, licking on these sad tits and telling me I'm the world: None of them ever moved me down where I was *made* into a woman by Jake Means. None of them. Not even Archie with his big, bull-black, proud self.

"But I wasn't about to buy none of Jake's religion. I knew about your daddy's churches. Was your father who turned me out in the first place when I was your age. Jake didn't know. I wouldn't tell him. He didn't know about the dope and whores your father was peddling right along with the gifts of visions, trances and healing at them church services. That boy was just a believer.

"I got me a pad over to Peshine Avenue. No more tricks. Jake used to work all day at Daddy's church and spend nights with me up in the apartment. He had the job of running the dining hall in the church, and he was paying my rent. He was even buying my coal. I was cooking greens and pork chops and keeping my man plenty of liquor; even got a job myself running an elevator in Bamberger's.

"Nobody knows how your father ran his churches and all his business. Like I say, I was one of Daddy's whores and I didn't know how it was arranged. I still don't know all of it. Jake was working for your father, and he didn't know nothing but the *amens* and *thank you Jesuses* down at the Broome Street tabernacle.

"Some people said it was a kind of hoodoo the way your

daddy did his business. I don't doubt it. God alone knows what all Daddy did or what he had, to make his name the way he did in this city—a half-black man coming here when he did in 1904. I know he told you it was 1927, but I had this fellah I know works for the city go downtown and get a Xerox paper what showed your father as the owner of Twenty-eight Prince Street in 1904. So if he came here in 1927, he'd been here before.

"Now, the way he made his church it wasn't like the Church of God in Christ or the Baptist Church or them Methodist churches. He *made* his church out of the scraps and broken furniture hanging out in the back of his mind. His church had a lot of the same things the other ones did (Jesus, the Bible, a choir, testifying, baptism—they sang the old Christian hymns, but there wasn't no Christmas or Easter celebrations), but everybody knew Daddy's church had something no other church had. It was all his, and nobody understood it but him. He called it the Metaphysical Church of the Divine Investigation. The people loved that church, maybe because you didn't have to understand it. People just took from it what they did. For some it was a healing. For others it was a financial blessing. Or it might have been victory over an enemy or victory over they own low nature. Or it was just being in that glittery large building on Sundays and Tuesday nights with all those people reeling and rocking to his voice and then dancing with the choir—dancing yourself out your miserable bones and flesh—dancing yourself clean for one more week. He started off that church in a storefront, and by the fifties it was the *United* Metaphysical Church with chapters over the world. Black and white was in it, some of them calling your father God Himself.

"That Broome Street tabernacle was the showplace of this city. It was tore down when you was three. Opening off the great entrance hall was the temple. On the ceiling was painted Moses' victory over Pharaoh's army. There was painted panels on the walls, and the floors was marble. Daddy preached from a high throne chair chained off and guarded so nobody couldn't reach him.

"You would enter the temple and an usher would take you down the purple carpet to your seat. The choir would be singing in a gold-framed stand, up in a gallery. Incense would be burning in brass bowls around the altar. Then, slowly the heavy purple curtains over the altar would come apart to show your father's throne, and behind it, raised up like a judge's seat, another chair, decked down with flowers and shining fabric, was the seat belonging to his mother, though nobody knew who she was, not even her name. They said she was always sitting in that chair, even though you couldn't see her and she could give you the wisdom to pierce the mysteries of the world.

"Gleaming gold cornets would blow, a gong would go to beating, and Daddy would appear in the back gallery, followed by his thirty lieutenants—all men. He'd have on a helmet like an old-time prince and a robe draping the floor behind him. He came all the way down and up to his throne in a procession with the people throwing flowers after him; and him walking heavy as God on the first morning of creation. First he would bow down to the chair of his mother, then he would climb the steps of his throne.

"People came to his church just as they was. They worshiped there at all different levels of understanding and for different reasons. Some people gave up everything to follow him. Others dragged in every now and then. Catholics belonged to his church; Baptists and Pentecostals. It wasn't denominational. Faggots was in there, whores, numbers runners, hit men—everything in 'the life.' Forty-eight-thousand-dollars-a-year lawyers was in there. So was doctors and, on occasion, in the dignitary section, different politicians and entertainers. Was a time down to the Orpheum Theatre in Newark when the owner couldn't get them jazz players to perform on Sunday till they'd all been down to the Broome Street church and caught Daddy's act.

"Daddy didn't have many rules in his church; once you was away from church, living your life during the week. All you had to do was tithe and receive his word. You could pay to have private sessions with him, and there was a time he sold cures and spells for everything from TB to love trouble. In the thirties and forties (and by the fifties in the mail-order section of negro newspapers and magazines) he sold magic powders and potions with names like Lucky Jazz, Get Away and Easy Life.

"He even sold a hair pomade called Wonder Fix what straightened our kind of hair better than anything on the market. He sold incense sticks for controlling and drawing spirits, love oils and sacred sands. Everybody bought some of Daddy's stuff. His motto used to be: 'When you tried *everybody*, and everybody fails, try *me*.'

"Daddy turned himself into a dream in this here city and entered the minds—in one way or another—of every man, woman and child.

"But in '62, time had changed too fast. We all looked and seen suddenly it was a whole new day. Daddy's game was looking old and run-down. The civil rights times had already started. Negroes was getting police dogs put on them in the South and marching and going to jail just for eating a damn hot dog next to some white person at a Woolworth lunch counter. There was this Prophet Elijah who was the leader of them first black Muslims. He used to wear a fez hat with a sequin star and crescent pasted to it. He claimed he met God in Detroit or someplace, and God said for the negroes to stop twisting they lips, ready to kiss the white man's ass, and build up they own nation and love they own black self and stop killing each other. He said even though Lincoln had freed the slaves, we was still in a mental slavery and had to stop eating pork, because even the New Testament show where the pig aint clean. Now, I could dig that, but I wasn't for joining *no* church, especially since the Prophet had set up all the regulations for his people, and women was separated from men in everything but making babies and couldn't straighten they hair or wear wigs—had to go natural and stay covered in white sheets, and I wasn't for that kind of mess.

"Then there was Malcom X, a fine-looking redhead nigger, and he was making real what the Prophet Elijah was teaching in a way the brothers and sisters in bars and on the street could dig. Yeah, he was where it was at. Martin Luther King was on the scene. He was getting through to middle-class negroes and the churchgoers.

"In the midst of all this, your father's organization—with all his mumbo jumbo—was starting to look more like a holdback than a headway. The Metaphysical Church of the Divine Investigation was getting pegged for a museum collection of handkerchief heads and hat-in-the-hand Uncle Peters. Plus rumors got going what was hard to hush—about how his big churches in Newark, Philly, Chicago and Harlem was fronts for narcotics and running bitches—which they was and always had been.

"It was April or May when Jake and some of the other young brothers working in your father's church started organizing to see what they could do about changing the reputation the church was getting on the street. They was meeting Mondays and Thursdays in the church dining hall, talking about the drug problem, juvenile delinquency, housing and so forth. They called themselves Operation ADVANCE and all the letters of the word ADVANCE stood for something. They got the cooperation of Reverend Blood, the one who was heading up the Newark district while Daddy was traveling. That little neighborhood concern group of Jake's was a thing what couldn't have never formed if it wasn't for the boiling times, number one, and the fact that your father was off in France, number two.

"Daddy was on a big preaching tour with that boy Sarah Anderson had in the fifties. Daddy had been using that child for a boy prophet, building up a whole new ministry around him, since the child was four years old, calling him a wonderboy and a holy guest in this world. It was Daddy's way of trying to deal with the new times, but it didn't work, and so he took the boy to Europe. That boy wasn't nothing. He was always a punk to his heart, and I guess that's the reason his mother and grandmother always kept him out of Newark in them private academies and places round white boys after he stop preaching. He looked like a hermaphrodite. His mother kept his hair long as a girl's. He had long eyelashes and delicate he/she hands. That boy—Emmett (I don't know if you would remember him)—was spoilt from the beginning. Daddy kept him dressed like a tiny emperor. His nose was always stuck in the air. I don't know where he at now, but he never caught on because most negroes couldn't stand him, and negroes was the biggest supporters of Daddy's church. That boy thought he was white. He might have gotten over with that shit in the past, but in the sixties, we was real sensitive about our color.

"But Jake's group was doing all right with the people, and when the other chapters found out what was going on here, Jake got in the position to call a big meeting with the district leaders; Reverend Blood was so impressed with him.

"I was right there with him too, wearing my little hats and Sunday dresses. They had me as one of the recording secretaries for the meetings. I still wasn't a member of the church, but I was Jake's woman, and he was my man. Plus my people was in that church, getting involved. Nobody never brought up any mess about me having been a whore either. Jake used to tell me about the Prophet Hosea God ordered to take a wife out of whoredom. And wasn't we all whoring on God, he would say: born in sin, departing from the truth?

"I watched that group of young black brothers come together

in June of 1962. They talked about what could be done to heal the slums in Newark, Philly and Baltimore, New York and Chicago. Them fellows put together a plan to get drugs out of the neighborhoods and put people to work rebuilding old houses the church would buy, providing day-care and nutrition programs, and working in a deep and meaningful way with the political scene. They plan was to be put to work throughout the American body of the church.

"When Daddy got back here at the end of June and found out about the ADVANCE brothers, he was furious. He wanted the one on the carpet who was responsible for all of it, and Reverend Blood gave him Jake. Jake was called to the house to Daddy's study late on a Sunday night, and I went with him, biting my tongue, scared I might lose my mind and try to take that place apart with my bare hands on account of what happened to my mother in that house. But I was cool. Peanut was cool. That was my first and last visit to Twenty-eight Prince Street.

"Daddy used his voice on Jake like a braided whip. He called my man everything but a child of God, and I aint said a word. I stayed cool, and it wasn't because of the bodyguards Daddy had with him in there either. It was because I knew if I let go I would have put my foot through a wall.

"Daddy was smoking them pencil-slim cigars then instead of his usual fat ones. He was wearing his hair cut short, almost bald, and he had on tiny wire-frame glasses. He said Jake was opportunity-happy and who did he think he was acting on his own? He said all them young brothers was going to have to withdraw they damn plan after I handed him over me and the other secretaries' misspelled notes and minutes. They might have been misspelled, but there was a lot of pride and love scribbled into them papers. Daddy flipped through them a tick and started ripping them up all over his desk. I thought for a split second I was fixing to get myself shot, I was so mad.

"'Then what we going to do about this situation?' Jake asked your daddy, humble as Jesus, and Daddy answered him, 'Not a goddamn thing.'

"I couldn't believe it to save my life, but Jake accepted what Daddy said. He sent Jake away from me to work at his mission in Haiti. I went to work at the Playbar, serving drinks, and your father got down to the business of filling his living room every evening with politicians, athletes, jazz musicians, artists and writers.

"People began to stay away from his church. The mountain of envelopes he got stuffed with prayer requests and donations was dwindling. And I hate to say it, but I rejoiced in my soul, because '62 was the year Daddy started to get what he deserved. He had a stroke in the beginning of August, and the grandmother, Sister Sarah's mother, took that hermaphrodite boy away from him. Daddy doted on that boy. I hoped he was going to die in the hospital they had him in, hooked up with a machine. Not only because he sent Jake away and told him he didn't want him around me no more because I wasn't no good—Jake didn't have to go if he didn't want to—no, but behind a whole lot of shit.

"I never expected nobody to understand how I felt over losing Jake, but my heart busted wide open. It looked like I was trying to drink myself to death. It might seem funny to somebody else; I'd only been with him a few months, and I didn't have no claim on him. We wasn't married. But it's more to a marriage than having the papers. It's a lot of people married has got the papers, still aint married. Look at Sister Sarah and her husband. Matrimony don't take place on the papers. Matrimony take place in the heart. I hear a lot of women say, 'Yeah, baby, that man is my meat, and the reason I know that's mine is I got the papers to prove it.' But if the papers all you got on your meat, baby, you going to be hungry. It take more than papers to keep a man. I loved Jake, and I believe he loved me, but when he say he was going to leave me and go to Haiti where Daddy had fixed for him to preach and be over the mission down there—when I saw that man had a heart and mind to follow your father over everything else in this world—I turned him loose. I let him go down to Haiti, where he could still be at for all I know about, because I went through my grieving like a magician walk through fire, and I come out the other side clean. I don't hold no hard feelings against Jake. I moved into this apartment right here on Quitman Street where I been for nineteen years. I been making my way for my damn self—and never had no one man to depend on. I been right here striving and reaching—gambling, baby—sometime look like I aint had nothing left to lose but my mind—and I'm still here. I'm still pushing.

"I'm not going to talk all day and night. I said I was going to tell you about your mother, and I'm going to quit when it's told. I want you to latch on to this thing the way it came down.

"It was a Friday just like it is now—hot like this too—when your father had that first stroke of his, and the annual convocation was supposed to start up on Sunday. Them week-long conventions was a big deal and brought out his whole church body to their mother church in Chatham, New Jersey, where he had his mansion what was photographed in *Ebony* and *Jet*. It was the one time of the year all the members of his congregation got to go out there. There was gardens with fountains and statues. He had horse stables and swimming pools. That's where your father's private plane was kept. The plane had his name written on both sides in gold, and it cost a thousand dollars an hour to operate. His cars was kept out there too—the white Rolls-Royce limousine, the Cadillacs and a 1937 Duesenberg.

"When word went out that Daddy had been knocked out by a stroke that Friday afternoon, most people took it for a sign and planned to stay away from the convention. The convention started on Sunday and moved along, kind of sluggish, night after night, Reverend Blood and a small group of church elders doing they best to stir up a feeling. A lot of church districts didn't even sponsor delegates that year or submit they annual dues to the convocation. Most people agreed your father had run a beautiful game, but his time was dead. A lot of them young brothers working with Jake was still around. They'd broke off from Daddy's Church of the Divine Investigation and was carrying on they plans on they own. One of them boys had already been killed trying to work with the police to bust a dope supplier out of Long Island. Some of the others stayed in the church and was instigating to take over the church from Daddy after the convention and run it the way they wanted. The convention ran out the week with the church over there in Chatham nearly empty.

"But when the news went around the next Saturday that Daddy had miraculously bounded back from a stroke, and was going to preach the closing Sunday message of the convention, women began to fry up chickens for paper-bag lunches, men rummaged the bottoms of they closets to look for they wing-tip shoes and cummerbunds. Children was stirred up. Everybody came. Sister Sarah and her mother was there sitting down in the front. I went on over there. Men had on they dust-blue and salmon-color suits with shirts and ties to match, ivory tie clasps and cufflinks. The women was wearing flouncy summer dresses and flowered hats. Little boys dug they hands in they vest pockets and swaggered. Girls with tight curled hair carried purses with nothing in them but Kleenex and a few pennies. We must have looked like a pageant flowing into them gates to the church grounds in Chatham and moving on into that big cathedral beside the mansion. We took over every pew and filled the three-tier balcony.

"But we brought a heavy attitude with us too. Daddy Poole was going to have to work hard for them *amens* and *yes lords* that Sunday, baby. His people was going to discern the spirits real careful, because they was afraid they'd been wounded—not by an enemy either, but by the very one they had loved and raised up above they self. Yes, they was going to discern the spirits, and if the right spirit came on them, the women might jump up and shake like candy to the pound. Somebody might say 'amen' and 'preach on.' But if no spirit moved them, your father's name was fixing to be dead on these streets, because them people what had followed him all them years was going to kill it. In beauty shops, lodge halls, poolrooms, they would burn up his name, just so they could breathe again. They would kill it just as sure as they had made it live and bloom bigger than life.

"So Daddy took his time. First thing we all noticed was that it wasn't no throne chair and his mother's chair was stripped bare. He stood in the lectern's light up on the altar, smoothing his pretty combed-back hair. Daddy surveyed the whole crowd like he was looking for faces and putting every face with a name in his mind. Then he threw back his head. For an instant, his face went pale, then the color come back. He parted his fine lips and smiled, and his gold-tipped teeth went to sparkling. Lord, he was pretty.

"'I know,' he said, 'that you have gathered under the sound of my voice this afternoon to witness some overwhelming event. Since none of you come to hear the Bible this afternoon, I won't weary you with the Bible. I'm going to give you what you come for. Daddy's going to give you what you really want.

"'I stand before you today, and I can feel the contentiousness in the room. Some serious charges have been raised against my character and against my leadership. I know there are those among you have already set the wheels in motion to bring me down from the head of this organization. Well, I want you to know this is my church. This is not a deacon church. This is not an usher church. It's my church. You are all sitting in my pews, under my roof, riding to Heaven on my coattail, so long as you followed my command. Now that time is through. If Reverend Brother Blood want a church, he'll have to go and build it. If this brother or that sister want them a church, they'll have to go build it. This is my church.

"'I started my church in 1927. I know the way every brick in it goes. Anybody crazy enough to fool with me don't know who or *what* they fooling with. Don't *nobody* know who I am. I slithered out of a crack of lightning one day. I made myself. Daddy Poole belongs to Daddy Poole.'

"Baby, he preached it, rearing back and holding on to that lectern. Looked like that man was going to slay us dead with words.

"'I am the whole vine,' he said, 'and you are the branches. He what lives in me, and I in him, will bring forth fruit, but without me you can do nothing. I built you a place to hide in your day of trouble, a tabernacle where you could offer sacrifices of joy, singing praises to God. Now you got to the place where you think you don't need me, where you restless and feel like you can do better. You don't tithe the way you used to. All our overseas missions are failing due to lack of money. We about to lose this building because we can't afford to maintain it no more.

"'I started this organization with the belief that if my effort would discover *one* good man, it would all be worthwhile. This afternoon, I look around me, I do not see that one man.

"'So, I am bringing an end to this United Metaphysical Church of the Divine Investigation, tearing up the charter— effective immediately. What money is left I am going to make disappear. You can all go to Hell. Daddy's through with you. And I'll tell you just where you can find me: number Twenty-eight Prince Street, Newark, New Jersey. I dare one of you to come near me. I dare you to cross my door. I promise to have something terrible and mighty waiting there on you—something to drive you out of your natural mind.'

"Then a billow of purple smoke washed up over the whole altar. We found ourself staring up at the ceiling trying to catch the last echoes of his big voice. When we looked back to the altar, the smoke was cleared. The holy magic show was over. Daddy was gone.

"He was in Europe for a while—in France, in that place called Montmartre. That's where he always seemed to go when he was reorganizing his game. I heard he had another stroke over there before he came back home, but you sure wouldn't have knowed it to look at him. . . .

"I was coming off an all-night shift, standing outside of the Playbar on Springfield Avenue, cussing out this little hatchet-head motherfucker I was going with at the time named Mink, when down the street come this long white limousine. The niggers all up and down the avenue was just going wild. It couldn't have been nobody but Sam Poole.

"I forgot what me and Mink was arguing about. I left him out in front of the bar with his mouth open. I was running so hard trying to get to Prince Street before Daddy got out of the car. By the time I got there, there was already a big crowd watching the car pull up to the curb in front of Twenty-eight. The driver got out first, then four big bodyguards, strong and ugly as sin. *Then* Daddy. We didn't know it was going to be our last good look at him. I was standing with a bunch of people on the short lawn out in front of Sister Anderson's house. She was out on her porch in her nightgown, so shocked to see your father, she aint even had time to have kittens because the niggers was standing all over her damn flowerbeds.

"Your father was clean as he wanted to be. A hush went over the whole street when he stepped from his big wheels. I swear he looked *superbad*. His marcelled hair was piled up in a six-inch pompadour, and he was sporting a red and black leopard-print suit—double-pleated, if you please—with high-heeled boots and a rhinestone bow tie. His blacked-out sunglasses was reflecting the streetlamps. Now, he had to be almost seventy-nine years old. But whenever your father came before the people, it was like he had a mojo hand against time. Daddy had the power to freeze his time like no other living man. He had gotten real thin, and I don't think I ever saw him looking so tall. All his movements had the force of a young stud's. There was five alligator-hide satchels—bulging big. The four bodyguards each was holding one, and Daddy had the other one. That's where he had the money—the money your mother left this world for laying her hands on. Your father wasn't never a person for doing business with banks too much no way. He liked to depend on bodyguards and hired guns. I remember when I was tricking for him—when I was his bottom woman—he could stuff half a million—five hundred thousand dollars—in fives, tens and twenties into a satchel like them he was carrying that dark early beam. I was to find out later that them satchels had brick-shaped blocks of gold in them—twelve million dollars' worth of eternal money. No way in the world you going to tell me that much money just disappeared.

"There was two police cars giving your father's limousine an escort, and that was just to show all us niggers that Daddy might have lost his churches, but he still had his high-up friends downtown in City Hall.

"But now what Daddy showed us next was the true show-stopper. This fine babe stepped out of those big wheels and took his arm. That was Miss Blanche, your mother, baby. She was a pure headlight, a real solid sender—lemon-skinned, black sapphire eyes, a round, full, red mouth, hair whipping back all down to her hips. She was long and cool, perched on high, dagger-pointed shoes, a twin fox scarf thrown over one shoulder.

"There was such a push and a moving forward trying to get a good look at her some people almost got crushed. The pounders had to get out of they squad cars and radio in for backups.

"Them dusty-butt whores and nickel-slick pimps was all checking her out. Everybody was checking her out, from doorways and windows, cars and all in the street. She was something to check out too. Miss Blanche's looks was a narcotic. He'd brought her from over there in his French stable in Montmartre—which from what I can figure is just a black ghetto in France—where he was keeping his finest bitches, and your mother was the cream of the sporting line. All them French black babes he had over there was the daughters of singers and high-class prostitutes what had ended up in Paris during the thirties.

"Newark was getting its first look at what them rich European white men had made your father famous for over there.

"Then Daddy tugged at her, and they all went inside Twenty-eight, and the police got back inside they cars and left.

"That's where they stayed—Daddy and your mother. That was about '63 or '64, the year you was born. Daddy had hired himself a little army. I never seen such negroes as the muscle-bound gorillas he had living with him in Twenty-eight—long wooly hair, two-toned liver lips and black enough to sweat syrup. First they was five (including the driver) showed up with him. Then in a few days, a few more came, and in another few days, a few more—like that—till they was a whole force—coming back and forth, carrying packages and food, guarding the house at night, sitting out in front of Twenty-eight in cars. Wouldn't none of them speak to nobody. Aint none of them looked like they was smart enough to say two words. They all wore black suits, and the leader of them, the one people went to calling 'Top Job' out of fun, wore a shark-tooth earring in his ear.

"I can tell you one thing though, nobody didn't fuck with them boys, and nobody didn't fuck with that house in no way, shape or form. After a while we just got used to them and the lights being on in Twenty-eight again, and Daddy and your mother passed four months holed up in there.

"It was winter when we saw Daddy or Blanche again. The car

would pull up in front of Twenty-eight in the early dark. First one of the gorillas would come out of the house and stand by the car. Miss Blanche would come out the house dressed to kill, with another gorilla right behind her, holding her overnight case. Them three would get in the car and drive off. That happened most every night until spring.

"I heard Daddy was whoring her to the baby-kissers and businessmen. That car was taking her to a house Daddy had set up in Union. Her johns was seeing her by appointment. They say she was bringing down four and five thousand dollars a night with the money he was charging for her, and he was using that money to work his way back on top, buying land. That's what I heard, I don't know, but if a woman ever had what it takes to be that kind of money-maker pulling flat-back tricks, just straight intercourse without nothing kinky, Miss Blanche was the one.

"Then I heard she got real sick with some female trouble and Daddy took her out of the life and had her treated at a hospital down in Philly. She recovered all right and they went on a trip somewhere. When they come back to Newark, she was big with you inside her.

"When Blanche got pregnant things seemed to ease up a little. Daddy let most of his apes go back to wherever they had come from, and you would see him and Blanche coming in and out more often, though they was always guarded.

"Why Daddy didn't just move off Prince Street, I don't know. He lost that place in Chatham, but he sure had the money to get far away from Newark. Maybe it was a pride thing. Then too there seemed to be something about that house had something to do with it. Don't ask me how I mean that. There're just some things in this world run deeper than words and some things can't be seen for looking.

"It was a long time after you was born before any of us got to see you. We just saw Blanche wasn't pregnant no more, and she was getting in that car again every evening.

"One night I was in the Playbar after we closed up, fooling with Longhead Pete while he was cleaning up. I was punching all my favorite records on the jukebox for free and half-counting my tips. I wasn't really in too much of a hurry to go home because that cold hawk wind was in the street, and I had quit Mink, and though his piece of car looked like hell, least it would always turn over and he used to pick me up after work every night. Longhead Pete aint never been good-looking, but he'd been patting and feeling on me and rubbing against me every chance he got since me and Mink had broke up. I was making out like I might give him a piece, but I hadn't made up my mind. This particular night, all I knew was that when Pete finished washing them shot glasses and things and handling the money in the register, he was getting in his brand new Buick, and I intended to get in there with him, because I wasn't *about* to walk to Quitman Street.

"We was digging Ray Charles on the jukebox and I was running my mouth about something, just as high as I could be now I was off work and killing a pint. I just felt like messing with Pete's mind, I guess. So I went around and closed all the curtains and checked to make sure the door was locked—which it was, because he always make sure he triple-lock the doors before he unlock the cash register. Wasn't no lights in there but the lights on the jukebox and the string of party-colored bulbs hanging around the liquor shelves. When Pete looked up and seen me coming from the windows he smiled and said, 'What you think you doing?' sniffing, all sexy and feeling hisself in the crotch.

"I came and sat up by him on one of the barstools and said, 'Wanna see something swift? Gimme a Kool.'

"He didn't know what the hell I was fixing to come out with, so he say, 'Come on now, girl. You know you don't smoke. Aint got no business drinking. You aint a well woman.'

"My heart always been bad. I had rheumatic fever when I was a girl, and I think that left me with a weak heart.

"I said, 'I aint doing so bad.' He give me a cigarette out of his shirt pocket then I said, 'Gimme a snapper.' So he lit the cigarette.

"So now I got the burning cigarette in my fingers, and I'm sliding back my skinny straight skirt.

"I thought that nigger was going to lose his mind.

"'Shit, girl,' he say in a scream-whisper, 'you aint wearing no damn drawers.'

"I got the skirt all the way back and opened my thighs. 'Show you something,' I told him. 'Little trick Daddy Poole taught me for them downtown fellahs when I was in the life. This here is what you call an educated pussy.' I brought the cigarette down between my legs and puffed it a few times with my pussy.

"Then I took it out and gave it to Pete to finish.

"He was down on his prayer bones in front of the barstool, begging me for you-know-what, when somebody start banging—BLAM, BLAM—on the barroom door and the windows.

"'We closed!' Pete hollered. 'Goddamn shit.'

"He was trying to get his mouth in between my thighs.

"I pushed him off. 'Wait a tick, Pete.' I always could feel trouble. 'It's somebody crying.'

"'What I care if they crying,' he said, hot. 'Let them go cry some damn where else.'

"BLAM, BLAM, BLAM!

"'I said we closed, motherfucker.'

"I jumped down off the barstool and pulled the plug on the jukebox. That made it darker in there and I went to the door, with Pete wrassling at me from behind. 'Hold off, dammit,' I told him, listening to the door. 'I aint hot now.'

"Was a woman crying out there. When I pulled the curtain so I could see what it was all about, my heart froze in my breast.

"I had to fight Pete off to get all them chains from the door.

"I was steady cussing. She fell into the bar. I held her up and stuck my head out the door to make sure it wasn't nobody after her. Then Pete locked up the door again and we brought her over by the bar so we could look at her good in the light.

"She was your mother, baby, and Daddy Poole had fucked her up. She wasn't able to tell me nothing that night. We made up a name for her and took her to City Hospital, and I made like I was her sister and she was visiting me from down South. Pete knew this babe what worked in the emergency room, and we was able to keep her 'accident' out of a report.

"When she come into the Playbar that night, you would have never known her for the headlight blew into town with Daddy Poole more than a year ago. All she had on was an old piece of bloodied gown—cold as it was that night—and blood had caked and froze on her thighs from where she said your father beat her in her pussy with a clothes hanger. Her eyes was two black swole-up slits. Her whole body was covered with bruises, where he done beat on her with his hands and his feet.

"Her right arm was broke in three places.

"By the time the hospital had her fixed up where she could go home, I'd made a place for her in my apartment. I went down to Springfield Avenue and bought a cot off the junkman. I fixed up a little crate for her to keep some toilet things in. Then I bought her a few underthings and a couple of housedresses. Her feet looked the same size as mine, and I had enough pinchers and stockings for the both of us. Besides, it was going to be a while before she could get around.

"At first I wasn't worried that Daddy was looking for her. That's how messed up she was. I figured he thought she was someplace dead. Pete warned me I didn't know what I was getting into, but I didn't want to listen. So he drove her over to my apartment one night after the bar closed and that's where she stayed for about eight weeks.

"After all that girl had been through, she was scared for *you*. She didn't know whether you was alive or dead. She told me her trouble started with Daddy Poole after you was born. He wanted a boy. She said he never laid a hand on her till after you was born. Before you came, all the while she was pregnant, it was nothing but him telling her a lot of big talk about all he was going to do for they son, how she wasn't going to have to pull down no more tricks, and how she could have anything she wanted for the rest of her life.

"But soon as she delivered a girl, he was making her leave you when you wasn't even weaned, back selling herself nearly every night. He couldn't claim you wasn't his. Your face was stamped with his face. Blanche said from the time you come in the world you always had his deep-set eyes and wide cheekbones, that same broad face, even if you did have skin darker than both of theirs and never had they good hair.

"Once she delivered you, your mother was a woman with no place left to go in the world. He aint want her for nothing. He didn't need the money she was making for him. He aint care nothing about getting back on the top of his game no more. He figured you was the last seed he had, and he wanted to make her suffer for not making you be a man-child, as if a man-child could have redeemed his filth.

"He was letting all kinds of men have Blanche now. Them coal-black guards of his was allowed to talk to her any way they wanted to, making all kinds of nasty jokes at her, and picking at her, talking about what they would do for her if Daddy ever turned her loose.

"One night up in Twenty-eight your father got hisself so piss drunk he was near 'bout crazy with rage and hurt over all the shadows what had gathered over his life. Blanche said in a year he'd started to bloat up from drinking hisself blind every night. He was already out his mind, Blanche said, performing some kind of rites three times a day, making candle offerings to gods

63

of storms and rivers and thunder—and shit like that—and had some old crazy woman coming in cooking for him once a day.

"He come into Blanche's room this one night where she was setting her hair getting ready to ride out to Union. He start talking about what a piss-poor excuse she is for a whore and a mother and how lucky she is he don't put his foot up her ass. You was next to the dresser in the crib by Blanche. He come and picked you up and hurled you over on the bed. You rolled, and just missed falling on the floor by this much. He say you his and he can do with you what the hell he want, eat you if he want to and put your damn bones out on the garbage.

"Blanche went into the dresser drawer and pulled out a shiv and told him she would stick it in his heart if he didn't get out of there and leave her and you alone. He shook his head like he was trying to wake up from a nightmare, apologized, laughed, said he was just playing with y'all, and soon as she put down the shiv he jumped her and beat the shit out her, then called hisself making love to her on the bed, with his stinking self, while she cried and held on to you by your little arms, dangling at the edge of the bed.

"He didn't mean your mother no good, but he wasn't going to let her leave him. Look like he had it in mind to just live with her till he killed her or she figured out a way to kill him.

"Daddy had that girl coming and going. He could have her busted for prostitution and her baby put in a foster home. Sure, he was the one who'd set her up out in Union, but she could have screamed on Daddy to the judge all she wanted, and nobody would have listened, with all the connections he had. Let her try to scream on him, and he could arrange to have her so doped up during her trial, till his lawyers and the court would cut her down, piece by piece.

"Plus she was in the country with no kind of papers—the way he brung her over here. She was *raised* in one of his damn brothels. Plus her English wasn't good. Daddy had her tangled up every kind of way. She was little more than a child herself. She didn't have no money. She didn't know how to even ride a bus by herself. He could kick her ass. He could kill her if he wanted to. She had to go for herself. She must have went over her plan a thousand times, then she closed her eyes and got on that tightrope.

"She seen him the next morning and she said she was sorry, but he didn't even remember beating on her. She thanked him for not hitting her in her face or bruising her and told him she hoped they could be more knitted together, promising to keep you out his way. She was so sweet with that man that morning till butter wouldn't have melted in her mouth. She was fighting the only way she knew how.

"When evening come, she laid out her things and ran her bath like she always did, just like she was going out to Union. She knew by trying to break free she was taking her life in her hands and taking yours in her hands too.

"She went in the bathroom next to her room (I never knew of your father to *sleep* in the same room with a woman) and ran her a bath. Then she locked her bedroom door and prayed he wouldn't knock on her door till she was gone. Daddy was down to two guards in the house by now, and one of them had the night off, partying with some of his reggae friends up in New York. The other one was down in the front room with Daddy watching a boxing match on the television.

"Her room was on the south side of the house up on the third floor in the back. She was hoping she could make it down the fire escape with you, then run, walk, hitchhike, make it any way she could, till she was out of Newark and could find a way to work and take care of you.

"Your father had made hisself a stash down in the cellar where he'd been saving up them brick-shaped blocks of gold he brought with him when he come back from Europe. The way I figure, somebody over in France was behind Daddy's game all along, though he was still the one always running it. When he had to close down his churches, he settled with somebody over there for the gold. Then he come back here and sold out the rest of his game to a syndicate. Anyway, Blanche had learned what board in the cellar he was stashing his shit under, and that afternoon, when him and his gorilla was out, before the beast-woman he had cooking for him come, she snuck down there and got herself a brick.

"She got down the fire escape and out that house, I'll say that much for her. She had on a satin gown and a full-length sable cape. Her hair was wrapped up in a turban. She had you wrapped in a silver fox stole, diaper bag slung on her arm. She was carrying a large envelope purse too and that's where she had the gold brick she aimed to cash in soon as she was somewhere safe.

"You can imagine how far she got wandering down Springfield Avenue looking like that before the men was hitting on her. She didn't have no money for a cab and probably didn't know how to hail one no how. Plus she sure couldn't pay a cab with a block of gold. She let this Chinese dude give her a ride, and he rode her right down to this abandoned brewery where Daddy and his nappy-black ape was waiting for her. The ape grabbed you from her, and the dude in the car pulled her in an alley where your father went to beating on her, beating her till he was sweating, and when he got tired of beating her with his hands he went to beating her with his feet.

"I made Blanche a promise that I would find out what had happened to you, and about a week later it came off the grapevine that Daddy had him an old white bitch living with him in Twenty-eight crazy about you, and they was dressing you up in all kinds of mean rags and buying you shit like money was going out of style.

"Blanche and me got to be like sisters, while she was getting better. I used to go to work at the bar then come home and talk with her till it was full light. We put your daddy's story together best we could between the two of us. She told me plenty I didn't know, and I hipped her to more than a few things. I told her everything my mother told me from when Mom was working in Twenty-eight—supposed to be maiding—the year before the Great Depression.

"Me and Blanche would talk, oil and plait one another's hair. Your mother was good at plaiting. We used to cook up a mess of food too, in that kitchen there what aint even big enough to fight a rat in. Blanche could cook a soul dish—smoked neck bones, black beans and rice and collard greens. Plus she showed me how to make tomato-rice-and-fish stew, and chicken in peanut sauce—*French* soul food. I showed her how to make liver and onions, chicken dumplings, sweet potato pone and grits with gravy—we had a ball, cooking for each other in here and getting fat.

"I was also doing my best to hip Blanche—to get her ready for when she got strong enough to get out here and make it for herself—all the different kinds of hustles to look out for. Me and Pete put our heads together and decided the best place for Blanche would probably be down South where folks was more slow and liable to take more time with her. We told her she might as well forget about getting you back. No way in the world she was going near Daddy's house without getting herself killed this time for sure.

"My mother had some people down in Baltimore—some first cousins—and I arranged for them to take your mother in and then help her to get further South. I helped Blanche with my own money. I didn't take no money from Pete. Getting her away from Daddy was something I wanted to do on my own. The night she left this town, we was both nervous as two nigger's chickens on Sunday morning. I fixed Blanche up in my new Persian wool coat and a wool hat what came down close to her ears. We walked down to Pennsylvania Station, going on just about every side street there was. It must have been about midnight when I put her on that train. I'll never forget my fine, headlight, high-yellow sister.

"That was it. Them relatives in Baltimore wrote and told me she wasn't on the train when they came down to pick her up. About a month later, I got my Persian wool coat and wool hat in a package in the mail. The hat had a hacked-off clump of your mother's hair inside it. The lining of my coat was all red as wine where it had soaked up and dried with blood. The night after I got the package, a Molotov cocktail went off inside Pete's little bar about two hours after we closed. Tore that place up. It could have happened with a whole crowd of people in there, but it wasn't meant to hurt nobody, so we figured your daddy got his point across.

"The place was insured, and that was when the Playbar got remodeled and the air conditioning was put in. Since then, we got a whole new setup in there and central air."

4.

≈≈ *M*artha stood, looking in her hands, by the only window in Peanut's apartment. She had not realized Peanut was done speaking, her mind was so filled with Peanut's voice. Peanut's voice was a whole musical band—rhythm and blues melodies, gospel chords, jazz riffs. She smiled like an amusement-house spook in serene suspension, humming and whining to the clear resonances of all her friend had said.

Peanut got worried. "What's the matter with you, girl? Come on away from that window."

She laughed—a bright burst that almost dispelled the room. Her head took on a regardant angle, leaning inside the window frame, then turned and lowered slowly to look down at the street, a flickering toy world getting ready for another Friday night. Tar-stained children zigzagged in the street, laughing at cars. Men dressed in loud tropical shirts and pegged pants were on the corner drinking wine, smoking cigarettes, eating barbecue, playing cards, snapping at passersby: "Hey, sister, you *wearing* them shorts." And, "Hey, cool, let me hold some change." Or, "Wanna cop some herb? This is some *righteous* herb." In front of Mr. Wonderful's Bar and Lounge the lacquered women had already begun to appear with their pimps though it was not yet dark, sitting in the back of Thunderbirds and Eldorados, *getting their gauges up*—smoking reefer, sniffing cocaine, sticking their thighs with homemade needles.

Martha could read the sign out in front of the canopied entrance to Mr. Wonderful's from Peanut's window: TONIGHT . . . THE STONE THRILLERS. That was Silk's new band. Peanut said you could hear those boys up and down Quitman Street once they started to wail. Silk had a funky new drummer.

She jerked from the window and walked out into the room. She took a hard, good look at the plaid-covered sofa where Peanut sat enthroned. Peanut's face struck a sphinxlike pose. The face seemed capable of holding that pose forever, the rigid, powdered-down face in a fretwork of light and shadow, the eyes drawn with eyeliner into thick Egyptian slants, so unreal Martha was startled when the face spoke.

"What the hell is the matter with you?" Peanut asked.

"I hope you know you late for work," said Martha nonchalantly.

"What do I care about late? If I don't get in there till closing time Pete better not mess with me the way I feel today. You act like you aint heard a word I said. Come over here."

Martha realized she was still holding the thin red scarf she had taken from the closet. Now she could not place in her mind her reason for taking it. She walked over to Peanut and laid the scarf like a garland over Peanut's head. She watched it flutter and rest on Peanut's shoulders and bony chest.

"You kill me sometime, I swear," Peanut said, using a fingernail to wipe a speck of lipstick from the corner of her mouth. "Your spirit been here before."

Martha was walking back and forth in front of the sofa, grinning to herself, watching Peanut out of the corner of her eye. Peanut looked at her with hunger and pride. Back and forth she went, slower each time, until she had Peanut hypnotized.

She stopped and said to Peanut, "What you want off me now?" unable to believe she had said it. She knew the answer to the question, but she would not have it played out this time without acknowledging what was going on, like those other times, with Peanut beating her down with words about her father until Martha did not know if she were living now or in the past, crowded by ghosts. Then being pulled down on top of Peanut in the thundering room; and Martha unable to whisper: *No.* How was she to know if any of the things Peanut said about her father were true, or what was true and what was a lie Peanut was using to turn her into a bulldagger? That was all it was— bulldaggering. Even if Peanut did still love men.

At first, she was only giving back some of the love Peanut had given most of her life, making little circles and spirals on Peanut's flesh, printing *thank yous* and *yeses*, holding on to another woman who knew her because she was a part of making her, and being held. Releasing herself in lightning flashes of pain, pleasure and heat. But the second time, she knew it had already become a habit. She could see it happening just like the first time, as if she were watching familiar streets pass from a speeding car on her way somewhere bright and forbidden.

A hard attraction was taking hold at Martha's root. Something in Peanut made Martha's spirit come flying free from the empty bottom of herself. Something about Peanut gave Martha to herself, wiser and more loving than she had ever known herself. Still she knew, because she remembered, that after she rose from the smells of the room and saw the light through the window turning ugly and vague, as night reached out to grasp Newark, pleasuring would turn to shame. She would still have to walk the mumbling, staring streets and pick up her baby from the sitter. She would still have to go home and face her father lying in the love-hold of death, and when she prepared herself for sleep, reaching out for her nightgown, everywhere Peanut had touched would be a mark, burning and real as a fire ready for her soul.

Peanut did not say anything. She got up and went into the bathroom. After the toilet flushed, she came out, her wig removed and an African cloth wrapped around her head.

"What's the matter?" she asked.

"I don't know," Martha answered, resolution leaving her.

"You scared?"

"Scared of what? What the hell I got to be scared of?"

Peanut crossed her matchstick legs and looked over at the window. "I was just wondering if you scared of me, that's all."

"I'm scared of myself if anything," she said low. "What I think I might do sometime if I don't bust loose."

"You a woman," Peanut said. "You grown enough to find the door if you don't like what go on in here. I can't force you to do nothing."

"I know it." She moved toward Peanut, stopped and said, "I just hate myself sometime."

"Don't talk shit, Martha. What you got to hate yourself for? You a champion every day you wake up in the morning and throw the covers off your face. You do what you want to do, hear? Grab all the love you can get, baby, off me or anybody else. You aint got no cause to fear me. My body aint nothing but a well-turned book. You can take this old love off me till you can get better. Lord knows you need somebody beside a baby and a father."

Peanut sat, watching Martha step out of the maid uniform. She opened the buttons of her blouse. The two women embraced, moving slowly to a singing that came from nowhere. Peanut tried to kiss her with her tongue, but Martha closed her mouth.

Peanut made such a forceful impression with all her big talk, her words crackling off like dried seeds in a pod, her flashy clothes and loud spirit, that it was easy for Martha to forget what she saw when she was this close to her—an aging ex-prostitute, with black-rimmed, drowned-out eyes, the rotten teeth, her whole body a route map of scars and healed-over burn marks.

She turned Peanut around gently on the couch, pulled away the blouse and rubbed her back. She stopped, fascinated by a long, furrowed scar.

She realized Martha was looking at the scar. "Life will mark you. I don't remember where I even got that now," she said nervously. "It disgust you?"

"No, Sister, it don't disgust me," Martha said, and she meant it. The scar looked like a bridge connecting one side of Peanut's back to the other. A strong bridge on which Martha could see herself moving, coming into life. How else was she here, breathing in this room, if not for the backs and visions of women like Peanut, playing their parts, supporting Daddy Poole down through the years?

She leaned her head heavily against the back of the couch. "Damn, I wish I had a cigarette."

"You aint smoked since you had Man."

"I started again; I been running so many changes behind my father." In one movement she was off the couch and putting on her uniform. She walked into the kitchen. She would have kept on walking were it not for the wall. She sighed and came back in the living room and sat down in front of the couch.

"You know something, Sister? I never had nobody once give me love without something else was on it. I'm talking about men—the only two I really known—Silk and Daddy. I aint even going to say nothing about this shit we been doing, because it's going to stop right now. Maybe Archie aint enough for you, but I aint no finger-artist freak. Be for real, Sister. What I need with another woman, when you got the same thing I got?

73

"I know how you love to run your mouth, and you still my girl, Peanut, because I sure as hell love you. But I can tell you shit even you don't know. You don't know everything about my father. It's like them holiness church women be singing on Sundays about God: *You got to know Him yourself.* And Sister, He's deep, *so deep you can't get under Him. So high you can't get over Him. You got to come in by the gate.* You might think I'm a fool because I don't use up the same number of words you do in a day, but I aint nobody's fool. I know who my father is, and I know what he is. I studied Sam Poole face to face. I learned him for myself. What I know about my father is fixed. It's like a city on a hill. You can't move it.

"I was only eleven when he started sticking his hands in my panties. Before that I don't remember nothing except crying all the time and always smelling like piss. I don't know how I would have made it those years if it wasn't for women who still believed in my father, leaving covered dishes of food out in back of the house where I could get them. Yeah, and if it wasn't for you, coming to get me and letting me stay over here with you when he would disappear for weeks some time. But there's one thing you left out in all you said about my father, and that's the way he went down after my mother left. He went down, Sister, and it was just like the slide was greased. I aint seen no goddamn bodyguards, no big cars. Farthest back I remember, Daddy drove a Chevy station wagon, and the engine in it was always blowing up, or the whole thing was breaking down. I grew up seeing my father messed up and looking like he was never going to get it together. They say you really learn a person when you know them in hard times, and I believe that's the truth about me and my father. I've known him to drag old whores up in that apartment and have them in the same bed I got out of, be drunk as a cockroach on DDT and raise as much sand as the Devil, but he wouldn't kill nobody. He love life—all of it. That much I know, so you don't have to tell me nothing.

"In my father's house I learned how to be thankful for everything I got and not to waste nothing. I didn't reach for a spoon unless the last spoon I used was clean. Was no cook. Plenty of times there wasn't no food. He'd made that two-and-a-half-room apartment for me and him in the back of the second floor. Sometime it be some little store or shop renting out the first floor. He'd rent out the other apartments to Puerto Ricans or Haitians. Other times it would be a whole lot of no good people that just broke into the apartments and was living there for nothing.

"When I came along Daddy didn't have no church. I was his church. Now here you trying to turn me against my father, telling me about some woman I never met, some shit that for all I know could be made up. Where is that swatch of hacked-off hair now? Why don't you show me your coat with the blood-stained lining? Maybe if you could show me that I might believe you, but all you can do is sit on that sofa and run your mouth. Far as I'm concerned, I came into the world without a mother, I mean that. You can think I'm jiving if you want to, but I mean that. I know Daddy wasn't no kind of father by a lot of people's standards, but he is the only father I got. I love that man, and he's real. What business he had grinding in me, doing the nasty and kissing me with his tongue when I wasn't barely old enough to know what the hell he was doing? What I know what business he had? Or why he did it. He did it because he did it, that's all. *So low you can't get under him.* That's a true song, Sister. I wasn't playing with children my own age. I wasn't half going to school, just enough to keep the state from taking me away from him. I was *living with* a man who was my own damn father. I didn't even know what I had till he told me it was a pussy and showed me how to push up to meet his thing, then pull down and rock back. I was his queen, that's all I knew, Daddy's woman. He used to bust open trunks out of the basement and give me old mildew dresses with beads and sewn-on pieces of mirror to wear, old horsehair wigs, face powder and feather fans to play with. He used to let me drink as much beer as I wanted, and sometimes, we be laying up in the bed and he'd let me take a puff off his cigar.

"I used to lay up in the bed and wait for him to come home . . .

"Then he started getting sick and he stopped fooling with me. He'd go out—by then wouldn't nobody even recognize him, though he was coming and going from Twenty-eight, it was like the Daddy Poole they was looking for just disappeared—go out, whore and drink for a week, then spend a month sick in his bed. The weight of his body growing bigger and bigger. His bloated face turned white, then plum-blue, then pumpkin-orange. He would take buglewood tea and treat his pox sores with myrrh till he got back on his feet. Then, after a few days, his weight would come right back down. That's how he always did right up to this last time.

"Come staggering up the stairs after midnight with a bottle of Beefeater's in each coat pocket. Carrying a big bag of porgies and trout in his arms. Fill up the kitchen sink with ice cubes for scaling the fish, then fry fish in cornmeal half the night till the sun came up. Singing all the verses to 'Stack O'Lee' a hundred times in his deep voice. Now that voice is trying to leave this world, and you want me to walk out on him. Leave him to die. Don't you know the world will heave up in the middle without Daddy Poole? Don't you know that much?

"Your problem is you want my father to be an ordinary man, and he aint. How you explain how he lived all these years in that house, coming in and out of Twenty-eight and nobody didn't even recognize him walking these streets—even you, Sister, or Sister Sarah? Or all the times junkies broke into the building and nobody never once cross the door of that apartment of his, even when I was living with Silk and had left Daddy there by himself? How else could he heal himself over and over with roots and herbs and sometimes with nothing but words if he wasn't from God and could lay down life and take it up when he want.

"My father is the true Christ, Ethiopian Jesus, a prophet under the law of love. He taught me black people are the only true Jews, the only real Israelites. We was the original people of the earth, the descendants of the union between King Solomon and Sheba, descendants of the tribe of Israel, descendants of Jacob. Jacob, God, Jesus, Moses and Esau was black. Blacks, not the white Jews, are the true people of the Bible.

"The white Jews are impostors! That's why they deny Jesus and refuse to follow the Old and New Testaments together.

"Daddy said we aint negroes or colored people or niggers or coons. None of those things don't even exist except in the mind of white people. The white man gave us those names when we was stole out of Africa and took away our true names, our wealth and our land. He taught us to fear the spirits—the only power we had. We are the true Hebrews, the children of Solomon and Sheba, the children of the living God. Daddy said the world is going to reel, and the nations will tremble. God, in His majesty, is going to enthrone the true Ethiopian man. We will go into all the highest places. The shrine of the black Madonna will be revealed. We will breathe on one another and salute one another with a holy kiss. People will live for hundreds of years. No disease. No hunger. All these things will come about because of the works Daddy performed out of the filth and dirt he found when he came to Newark in 1927. Because of the ground he laid for the lost to turn to God."

Martha broke off, breathing fast.

Peanut got off the couch and came over to Martha. She slapped Martha so hard her long flat breasts shook and her turban came undone. She reached up and covered the sparse white braids on her head. Her hair was thin from years of straightening with grease and a hot comb.

"Baby, you out of your mind. You have snapped your damn cap. That's the shit Daddy taught you? I'd be too shamed to tell anybody I believed that shit. What about the time he had you around there getting ready to sell your ass? You come running over here to me, and I helped you. You mixed up, baby. You aint right. Your father is crazy. The sooner you admit *that* to yourself the better off you be."

Peanut turned and walked back toward the couch.

Martha felt cold and hot. In an instant her broad, shiny face came to life. Her head pounded. Screaming, she leaped from the chair and pushed Peanut into the back of the couch. She had her hands around Peanut's neck, pushing and tightening. Peanut stared into Martha's dilated eyes, gasping for air and trying to get her hands into the folds of the couch.

"Awright, bitch!" hollered Martha. "Awright, motherfucker. I had enough! You hear me, bitch? You hear me?" she screamed into Peanut's amazed face. She shook her and screamed, "You hear me, bitch?"

Peanut worked her hand down into the cushion and grabbed her knife. When Martha saw the knife come gleaming up from the couch, she went berserk, bringing her knee furiously into Peanut's chest. She wrenched Peanut around and twisted her arm behind her back.

Peanut gave up a weak cry and dropped the knife on the floor. She doubled over on the couch, holding her arm across her chest. Martha grabbed the knife and shook it at her.

"Awright! Now, *I* got the knife. Come on and fuck with me. Come on, bitch, and try me. Run your mouth now. I dare you. Come on."

Peanut groaned and struggled to her knees on the couch. She lay back and fixed the turban, watching Martha.

"Your big problem," Martha said, "is you just want Daddy to be an ordinary man. He's a spirit man, and that's what make him too deep for you to understand. The spiritual always been the most important thing to him. So what, you been his whore. You know what you know. Plus what your mother told you, you say, from when she was the downstairs girl in his house back when Savannah Sparks was his woman, *you* say, because he never said *nothing* to me about Savannah Sparks, and I know it's a lot probably he aint said nothing to me about, and I don't want to know about no way. But awright, Sister. Still and all, it's mighty funny to me then, even after what your own mother told you about Daddy and what you say happened to *her* in his house, you still went ahead and was one of his whores, since I don't remember you never saying nothing about him *making* you be his whore. Whatever it was about my father that made you want to fool with him, even after your mother told you a lot of shit about him, *that's* the power in my father I'm talking about. What he is, you can't say he's wicked or good. I don't care if you thought Daddy was crazy, evil or divine, girl—you still had to check him out for yourself, didn't you? Everybody's got to know my father for their self. He got something no other man has. Had it then. Got it now, laying up there in that second-floor walk-back on Prince Street. He pulled you to him and still pulling you to him. That's how come you all the time talking about him and calling his name even though you say you hate him. You can't help yourself for loving my father. All I can hear is how you still love him in everything you say. If he sent word by me right now the voodoo was off his door, and for Sister Peanut to come to him, you would come."

"I wouldn't," said Peanut, sitting sideways on the couch. "I hate the sonuvabitch. I thought I loved him when I was young, but, shit—"

"Shut up! Just shut the fuck up, bitch. Yeah, you older than me. Seen all kind of times that I aint, but if I got to live all the years you lived to wind up being the stupid bitch you became as far as what Daddy is, I rather take this knife and give up my life right this minute.

"You got to understand my father. You can't envy him if you want to understand him. That's the first thing. No way in the world you can *be* Daddy. You *have* to serve him. You *have* to come in by the gate."

Peanut gave her a void and patient look. "I just want to know why you didn't 'serve' him when he tried to put your pussy on the street? And once you got yourself clear of him, why in the name of hell you come back to him? That's all I want to know."

"I'm getting at just that thing, Sister. That's what I was trying to tell you when you slap me in my damn face."

"That aint what it sounded like."

"I don't care what it sounded like to you. I said I was getting at it and I was."

"Then give me that phone and put that knife in the kitchen where it belong. I'm sick of playing kid's games."

Martha hesitated, then picked the white Princess phone off the floor and sat it on the couch. From the kitchen, she could hear Peanut on the phone with Pete at the Playbar, saying she was not coming to work tonight, saying her blood pressure was up.

She came back into the living room and sat, facing Peanut.

Peanut was still on the phone. "Look, I'll work an extra day for you next week. I don't care who you hafta call, I aint coming in. I don't care if it is Friday night. My blood pressure jumped up, and I can't see my doctor till Monday. Yeah, I just got off the phone with him. He say take it easy till he look at me. He going to have to put me on a new prescription."

Peanut went on, making up lies, then she and Pete started talking about people who came into the bar: "She stay high half the time anyway. You see what she had on the other night. She look like she was from outer space."

Martha looked over at the framed snapshot sitting on the cocktail table beside her. It was a photo of Peanut and Archie taken in Atlantic City last summer. Archie was about seven feet tall and as black as a world full of midnight. He was younger than Peanut and always wore Converse sneakers with colored strings. Archie had wanted to be a national-league basketball player, he said. He had been an orderly at Martland Medical Center for eighteen years.

In the photograph, he hugged Peanut and grinned. Peanut had on a long, white-fringed top over white slacks, a gold lamé jacket, a short, auburn, "jerri curl" wig and a pair of open-toe pumps. She was smiling a black mama alligator smile, looking off.

Martha wished she had a cigarette. She started smoking when she was thirteen. She had smoked a pack a day for three years. She quit the same day she quit Silk; gave up being his fool the same day she gave up the cancer sticks. Now she was smoking again. She had already finished the pack of Kools she bought on her way from work yesterday.

"Yeah, Pete, you take it easy then. I'll pick up my check Monday on my way from the doctor's office. Okay, baby. See ya later."

Peanut hung up and put the phone on the floor.

The women stared at each other. Finally Peanut looked off— like her last summer's self in the snapshot—and said, "Whip it on me now, sugar: Talk."

5.

*"Jelly Roll killed my momma
and drove my father mad . . ."*
—BLUES

〜〜 "The first time he did it to me, and I bled, he said I was the whole earth, and he was the sky. After that, he said it so many times, till I was saying it to him. I'll be damned if the whole earth wasn't what I didn't look like laying up in his bed in old mirrored dresses, with fake red hair spread out over the pillows full of silk flowers and little combs made out of seashells and crystals. My face would be all painted and powdered. I had on rings and bracelets and beads. Laying up in the bed, un-washed, smelling like sex and powder and, sometime, like blood.

"I didn't know my father in his religion-business days. I knew he was a preacher. He told me himself. 'Now, I just preach the blues,' he used to say, 'deep in debt to the Devil.' I know he used his churches to front his whore racket and an illegal gam-bling bank. I know because he told me. Told me a lot more besides. He wasn't shame of what he did. I also know there was power in those churches of his, and the people would come and throw money on his altar, thanking him for the sight he gave back to their eyes, the hearing he gave back to their ears, and the feeling restored to their legs. Cured their soul-sick conditions. Breathed the spirit back in the barren darkness of their souls. That's how *he* talked. More than all that, he showed them a *man* they could believe in, a *man* that could lift up all people and carry them on up to the tip-top of the world.

"From what I know about religion it's all made out of good and evil. Good and evil give out and break right down where my father begin. Daddy used to tell me, 'All the things I did, were done because one day, long time ago, Jesus Christ was born, and He lived and died and rose from the grave. These works are justified by His death, burial and resurrection.' Now *that's* religion, but the world aint come to it. It's far ahead of people, going to church looking for handouts from God, singing songs they aint thought about, celebrating Christmas and aint realized Mary had to have her baby by *somebody* and it sure as hell wasn't her husband. It's ahead of the other people too going to bars just as religious as saints go to church, calling themselves mad at God and living a no 'count life. The religion I got I know is real. It has nothing to do with good or bad, being in the world or being in the church. I got it when I was eleven years old. I got it laying up in my father's bed. You think I must be out of my mind. I might be, if out your mind is where you got to go to get truth.

"Everything I am, and everything I know, comes from Sam Poole. From his words and deeds and what he put up inside me through his sexing me and loving me the way I know now no father aint had no business doing but didn't know then. He made me as much woman as you when I was eleven years old. As much woman as walk down these streets. Made me old as stone and hard. Yeah, I aint going to say it didn't hurt me when I got to where I could understand what he was doing with my body was wrong in the world's eyes, and how come it had to be a secret, but I still wouldn't be nobody else but Martha Poole or Sam Poole's daughter.

"If I had to stand him taking sex off my half-made body in order to get his love and his truth, I would go ahead and stand it again a million times. I'm not ashamed to say it. I don't care what people would say about me or my father, or what some caseworker would think. Or some damn religious person. Or no hip person neither. Time was I would care, but not now. The reason I don't usually talk about my father is because what happened between him and me belong between him and me. It aint nobody else's business. What you say about Daddy and all he did, that's on you. I know I had it hard trying to grow up, but there was a miracle wrapped in it, and I wouldn't had it no other way. I *know* I earned my seat in Heaven. Plus I earned the right to show my son the way through this world.

"When Daddy started getting sick, he didn't mess with me no more, but before he stopped having me in his bed, he taught me about how the world was made and how to get power and who he is and all about when he came to Newark in 1927. He taught me about his mother too, only she wasn't a spirit sitting on no chair in a church. He called her Mozelle. It was her clothes he went down in the basement and brung up for me to wear, her powder and beads and fans.

"He never said the name Blanche to me once. If my mother was any kind of woman, don't you think he would have spoke her name once in all this time? He just said the mother I had birthed me just like a dog and moved on. He said she was dark-skinned with short, tight hair, kind of stout and straight-legged like I am now. Outside of saying that, he skipped right over her. But my grandmother, Mozelle, the Mother of All, he taught me plenty about her.

"Sister, I know a lot you don't know and aint slick enough to make up. My father was the son of a whore, but Mozelle wasn't only a whore, she was the mother of whores. That's what he called her: *Mother* of Whores, like she was somebody to always be proud of. He could lay next to me and talk her up so clear I would almost see her with her light skin and dark hair. I could almost smell the Persian incense Daddy said she kept burning in that house of hers on Avon Avenue. A big, near-white woman, Mozelle was living by a hundred different names. She was 'the Black Diamond,' 'the Empress,' 'Red Lightning' and other names Daddy told me that I can't remember. He said she was what people in New Orleans called a marabou, and that's where she was from, down there where they had two kinds of negroes— regular negroes, like the ones you see nowadays, and near-white negroes, marabous, that could speak French good as a foreigner and lived in big houses, with blacks waiting on them hand and foot, just like white people with money.

"Mozelle, she came up here from New Orleans before your mother was born, and Mozelle was one of the biggest whore-house queens on the East Coast. She was making big money and skimming off the top to pay the police for protection. She didn't deal in nothing but fine, almost white girls, and she had plenty of them in service at her place on Avon, strutting through the fancy parlors to old-time jazz music, wearing nothing but rhine-stones and feathers. Downstairs in the basement, Mozelle had a big gambling room where her Italian rumrunner boyfriend and a whole lot of Dago pretty boys used to sit and play roulette when they aint feel like fucking. Mozelle got to be so rich she used to decorate the walls in her bedroom with horseshoes and Stars of David made from emeralds and diamonds. All those jewels she had were presents from the big white men that came to her whorehouse.

"It was Mozelle who brung my father to Newark (where he was right before that he never said or maybe said to me before I was too young to understand, because even though I didn't start laying up with him till I was eleven, I can remember him always telling me things about the mysteries, Mozelle and who he is, all my life like he was laying a foundation). It was her, Mozelle, who helped him set up his churches here, helped him get hooked up with her rumrunner boyfriend, because in that time, dope wasn't the thing, it was liquor. Liquor was illegal. So in the beginning, that's what Daddy's churches was fronting for: a prostitution game he took over from Mozelle, and he was facing for the rumrunner too. Later he took in the numbers game, but that was because once he started making a name, people was always writing him and sending money, asking for numbers to play. He used to work it into his radio ministry program. He would preach a certain number verse out the Bible, like Luke 6:38, and that would be the number: 638. And all those numbers players that was hitting left and right off Daddy's numbers would tithe and support keeping him on the air, but he was getting so many envelopes with cash and money orders he could have bought ten radio stations. That's when he decided to start his own gambling-policy bank."

Peanut was sitting on the couch with her chin drawn in and her neck back. She had a large glass brooch holding together the center of her turban. She was wearing her "reading glasses," which she put on whenever she read the newspaper or TV *Guide* or whenever someone was telling her something important.

She had been staring with dead aim into Martha's mouth. The girl's mouth moved like it was forced to function, forced by words that did not even sound like her own.

Martha was like some storm-driven bird giving out a song in the dim, still, hot room. Martha's words were filled with rushing melodies, playful runs, crescendoes and breaks. Peanut waited until there was a full-measured stop and, before Martha could pick up her next note, interrupted.

"Hold on a minute," she said, and spit into an empty beer can. "You say your daddy started his churches fronting for a whore game he took over from this woman, his mother,

Mozelle. If he took it over, where did *she* go and what did she do?"

At first she thought Peanut was trying to trip her up as if she were lying. "I don't remember nothing about where she went. I just know Daddy took over his running women from her, because he said so. Before he came here, he loved women good as he ever did, but he'd never thought about putting none of them to work for him. That was in the mother's plan. She had it all laid out for him when he got here. He used to tell it over and over. How he could have a church here, and how the Italian boyfriend was going to kick in so much money, how my father would sport the babes, and how Mozelle would fade from the scene. That's what I know. Just how she faded or where she faded I don't know."

Peanut lifted her arm and pointed at Martha. The flesh shook beneath Peanut's bony upper arm. "I know right where she went, baby. And your father *still* aint worth the powder it would take to blow his ass to hell! It was Montmartre, baby, sure as you born."

"How you get that?" snapped Martha. "You don't know nothing about the mother. You sat here and said yourself you thought she was just a spirit sitting up in a chair at my father's church. Mozelle was before your time. Before your mother's time. You have said yourself a hundred times to me and I have heard you say it before other people that your mother didn't come to Newark till the year before the Depression."

Peanut looked indignant. "That still don't stop me from hearing about this near-white madam—used to just call them *landladies*—what had a cathouse supposed to be so great on Avon Avenue. It wouldn't have stopped my mother from hearing about her either since it wasn't long after 1927 that she came to Newark. Only I never heard nothing about this landlady being the mother to Daddy Poole. She had one more name: 'the Jewel of Newark.' And sitting here just now listening to you talk it come to me: Who else could be the mother to the evil Sam Poole fathered in this city?

"It come to me right when you was talking about the diamonds and shit on her walls, it *would* be her, the black-white lady I heard talk of when I was a girl. And what your father look like but a black-white man? It aint all that much I heard about her except what she was and how the white men loved her and this: that she kept a snake under her bed she used to feed just like a baby, because, you know, snakes supposed to love milk. I don't know if it's a tale, but that's what people—old people— used to say about her. She was gone from Newark before I was born, and where she went was Europe—France. She flew out the Newark Airport when it was brand new. It had to be Montmartre, the same place where Daddy got your mother from and brung her here to have you and then slaughter her dead as a side of meat."

Martha dismissed Peanut's statements with a cool glance to the side and said, "I just say what I said about Mozelle and all that to show where my father came from, and that he got using women the way he did from his own mother. So, it came to him natural, and that's why he made it a part of his vision. You can say it was a demon vision or a vision from God, but the thing is it was a vision with power. It was a vision my daddy was big enough, bad enough and *man* enough to act on. One hundred years from now, it won't matter if my father made money off negroes trying to hit a number, or if he had whores, or none of the shit people say about him.

"My father taught love as the guiding spirit of the universe, and he taught knowledge of the low and the high self. You didn't have to understand him to receive his truth when he was a preacher. He said his truth wasn't so much in his words as it was in the sound of his voice. He wasn't an ordinary man.

"Daddy taught love, and for him, because he's from God,

there's no difference between his low self and his high self. I have the understanding now I once didn't have: that my father wasn't using me for sex, and he didn't *need* me to turn tricks for him. He was trying to teach me about divine love.

"All that's going to matter is the work Daddy did in these cities and over the world and the truth he put inside us. Won't nobody know or care how he done it. And he'll still be living, too, because his *nature* can't die.

"Don't misunderstand me either, because I appreciate everything you done for me. You helped me when I left Daddy. You helped me after I had Man. You and Archie went and bought all those baby things. I didn't have to ask you for nothing, you just did it out of the goodness of your heart, and I appreciate you for it. But I want you to know, much as you say you hate my father, what I appreciate you for the most, Sister, is the time you spent being one of his whores, helping my father's dream, even though you don't understand it. I appreciate you for that, and if he didn't never say thank you, I want to say it for him right now: Thank you, Sister. I know my father is a great man, but I also know you can't have a tabletop without the legs. There aint no king without the people. So I thank not only you but every woman that supported my father and his dream in any way, shape or form. You didn't like the role you had to play for him, I know it. I didn't like mine. How you think I feel now twisting them sheets on his bed and scraping his shit into the toilet, but I do it. I do it just the same. You don't have to *like* your duty to be a soldier for God. All you got to do is fight till you die.

"My father used to say to me, 'Babygirl, I didn't mean my women a bit of harm. It's the same word, understand, Baby: *tricking,* meaning conjuring, witching, spell-weaving; and what the whores do, *tricking* with johns. All my women was on a mission, Baby, to raise up the nation. Don't never let nobody tell you different.'"

Peanut looked at Martha with contempt and love turning to

pity in her eyes. "Daddy is sure a man," she said, "what is going to weep in his dying hour."

"But, yeah, I walked out on my father," Martha went on. "I was thirteen years old, and, far as I was concerned, I was grown. I looked grown too. I was keeping myself clean for the first time in my life, and if he ever came in there and fell asleep with any money in his pockets, I could go out and shop and cook for myself. I was wearing Kotex. I was carrying a pocketbook. Hell, I was grown. He hadn't laid a hand on me to kiss me or pat my ass or nothing in, I'd say, about a year. I still aint had no interest in boys, but I had girlfriends, now that I was going to school more regular and didn't look so much like a total freak like I did before. Those girls would talk about sex, although they aint know shit about it. I wouldn't say nothing, just listen to them talk. It was through finding out they were virgins and hearing them talk that I began to really understand I was ruined by my father. So when he come in the house early one Sunday morning with this old, greasy paper bag with some plastic shoes and some stupid plastic flower in it and come telling me I was going on the street wearing that shit and get in men's cars and suck them off and pull their meat carrying on for ten dollars a ride, I told him he was a motherfucking liar. I told my father he could kiss my black ass.

"He didn't say nothing. He was half drunk and sick. He just stood in the living room looking at me like I had shot him and he was waiting to feel it. Then he went on in his room with his greasy bag and went to sleep.

"I went right on about my business, going to school and trying to be like other girls. I was even learning how to do something with my wild hair keeping myself neat and clean, but every weekend he kept coming in, laying hints about the nice change I would pick up for me and him if I would get out on Springfield Avenue or down on Market Street where they have them porno stores and get in men's cars. Telling me how he would give me a can of Mace so I'd be covered if one of my johns tried to pull some mess on me. I knew none of my girlfriends' daddies wasn't talking to them about no johns or giving them no Mace either. I still had never said a word to him about him fucking me, so I was just letting it all ride, and just hoping he would stop talking about me turning tricks and I could just go to school and pretend I wasn't different from other girls.

"But one Sunday morning he come in and pulled me off the little cot I had set up in the living room to sleep on. I'd stop taking the chance sleeping in his bed when he wasn't home, stopped taking that chance a long time ago. He come and pulled me out of the bed, and I'm standing there in my bra and panties, rubbing the sleep out my eyes. I look and see he got some big old—I don't know what—look like some kind of nasty, dribble-lipped cracker old enough to fart dust, wearing garage overalls. He come telling me to go with him. 'Put on something, Babygirl, and go with this gent'man.' I thought I was getting ready to leave this world and take both of those men with me. I started grabbing and throwing things in that room. I hit my father with a candlestick and knocked him out cold. That old cracker must have thought I was having a damn seizure he got out of there and down the stairs so fast. That's when I packed my little shit—a comb, my toothbrush, two dresses, some underwear and my Chaka Khan record (even though I aint had no record player)—and came over here. I turned fourteen and fifteen living in here with you.

"Then I met Silk—Ralston Melvin Edwards—and he was Daddy Poole all over again, just in a different way, but by then I'd been away from my father long enough that I wasn't mad at him. I kind of missed him. I'd even go by sometime and if he didn't have some old bitch up in there with him, he'd hand over a dollar and ask me if I was doing okay, if school was all right, and tell me to listen to my teachers.

"Silk never actually looked like Daddy to me—just good-looking, that's all, and older than me. I never knew him not to have his hair in a process no matter how messed up he got, even if he had holes in his shoes or his clothes was ripped, and that would be rare, because Silk is one black man that loves to rag. That's how he got his nickname he told me, because he was always wearing some boss silk vines when he wasn't nothing but eleven or twelve. His mother still lives on South Orange Avenue by West Side. His father killed himself when Silk was little, and the mother lost her mind. They say Silk is the spitting image of his father, and that woman aint had no better sense than to spend nearly all the money she had buying Silk all kinds of expensive clothes from New York. He used to look so fine in elementary school till he *had* to learn how to fight because the other boys was always calling him a faggot.

"First time I ever knew anything about Silk I was walking up Charlton Street with my girlfriend Liz, this widemouth girl I used to run with. Liz went to Barringer and we met at a social me and some of my girls was at. Liz and me was on our way over to her house to listen to records and practice dance steps. It was Saturday, and first we would help Liz's mother clean up their apartment although you couldn't never make that place look clean no how, but after I helped Liz do her housework we could listen to music on her mother's four-speaker stereo and do the 'robot' and 'freak' the balance of the afternoon.

"We was coming up Charlton and got right to West Kinney where we always turn to go to Liz's because she lived in the projects (I heard she moved to Atlanta and got a job as an airline stewardess now) when this smoky-dark, fine-looking man with a red suede jacket lean over in his car and said, 'Hey, baby, you want to ride?'

"Now, me and Liz seen him at exactly the same time, but we kind of looked real fast and kept walking. I really didn't think he was talking to me, not that I thought Liz was all that much better-looking than me, but I just never really thought of no man close to my age being attracted to me.

"So, we was stepping right past him in his red and black Trans Am when all of sudden we hear this horn blowing mad, and don't you know, that nigger opened his door and got out and hollered all loud, 'Hey, baby, what you doing for it?'

"I aint even know what that meant, I was so square. Me and Liz was stopped at the curb, but we still aint turn around. We arched our backs, then we laughed. I whispered to Liz: 'What do "What you doing for it?" mean?' 'It mean what it say,' she said: 'What you doing for *it?*' 'Well, what the hell is *it?*' I still aint know. 'His dick, stupid.'

"I was so shocked I turned around and looked at him without even realizing. That was when he caught my eye and smiled. 'Yeah, you the one I'm talking to.' I could have fainted dead in the street. Liz was turned around too, with her mouth hanging open like a busted gate. I grabbed Liz's arm and said, flirting the way I used to play at with Daddy, 'I'm going somewhere with my girlfriend.'

"Liz looked at me. Then she looked at Silk. She looked back at me. I could hear what she was thinking without her saying it: *Girl, you crazy?! Here this fine—and I mean fine—nigger with a car asking you to go for a ride, and you talking about going someplace with your damn girlfriend! You better get in that car or I will.*

"He looked at me for a long time, and I just stood there next to Liz to make sure he got a good look. Then he said, 'Maybe another time.' And I said, 'I don't know, maybe.' He went to get back in his car. He said, 'I'll catch you later,' but it just sounded like 'I'll catch you' to me. Then he drove off.

"I had to listen to Liz going on and on about him all the rest of the afternoon, about wasn't he cute, and didn't he have on some nice rags, and did I check out that sharp car? And what was the matter with me, was I turning funny or something, passing up a chance to ride with that boy? I told her I didn't know nothing about him. She said I could see all I needed to know from where I had been standing. I didn't even know his name, I told her. That's when she really got off. His name was Silk. He was nineteen. He was taking college courses downtown at Rutgers. She had a cousin who lived around his way. Silk hung out at the New Deal Poolroom over on Livingston Street off Springfield Avenue. He worked for his uncle in a candy store, and she told me right where the store was in case I wanted her to go by there with me one day after school and see if he was there. She said she heard he was a musician or a writer, something deep anyway, and I was a fool if I didn't take advantage of a boy like that liking me.

"I just said I couldn't see how him wanting to know what I was doing for dick had that much to do with liking me. Liz said I was young and didn't know nothing, even though I was three months older than her and could have told *her* things about men, if I'd wanted to brag, but then she would have known my secret. Still and all, I had to admit Silk made me feel strange standing out on that street with his eyes moving over me like I was a girl in a porno movie. Standing out there with his eyes turned on me like that and his mouth curled in a smile I never seen on nobody before, nasty and sweet mixed up together. Yeah, I had to admit I had felt my scalp crawl up and my chest raise and my ass sort of sling back, getting all comfortable and good-feeling. If that's the way your body tell you its ready for a certain man, I guess mine was telling me Silk looked like the negro for me.

"It wasn't long after that I began to burn, up and down the streets of this hill, looking for Silk everywhere. I wouldn't say nothing to him if I'd see him; I'd just look at him, bottom to top, and keep on moving, whether he saw me or not. Plenty of times I saw him with the boys that was in his crowd at the New Deal Poolroom. Sometime I'd see him sitting up in a steak shop with some girl stuck in his face—older girls with the bodies and the hair I'll never have. Lot of time though, he'd just be by himself, driving in his black and red Trans Am (if he stopped and offered me a ride, I'd say no) or walking fast through the street carrying his sax (then it was a baritone saxophone, before he switched to a tenor sax, then the alto sax) on his way somewhere to play a song, I imagined, that made him think about me. I couldn't get my mind on nothing but Silk, Silk, and some more damn Silk. I wasn't doing good in school. I aint have my mind on studying. I would be sitting in class drawing pictures of him in the margins of my textbook, not listening to a word the teacher said. If I saw Silk with another girl I'd get so sick in my mind till I couldn't eat. I wouldn't go to school. I'd just walk around the game arcades and department stores downtown humming some candy ass love song I got off the radio. I wasn't seeing none of my friends.

"The way me and him finally got together was I was at the point where I knew I had to talk to him or go walk in front of a moving bus, I was that much half in this world and half in a fantasy. I went into the store where he worked. There wasn't no customers in there, just his uncle sitting by the door playing with this little girl with long braids. I aint had a bit more mind of what I was going to say to Silk then if he was a movie star. I must have looked like a zombie for real, coming in there with my old pocketbook hanging off my arm, staring, no kind of expression on my face. I just went up to him at the counter and stood there, like I was waiting.

"Finally he let out a big laugh that shook me clear out of my love dream and said, 'Girl, you so full of pussy I could smell you coming.' Said it all loud and happy. His uncle over by the door went to laughing. Even the little girl was laughing, even though she aint had no idea what the hell she was laughing at. Shit, I laughed too. I guess he had to say something, and that was good as anything, because I wasn't hip enough to say nothing, and that's how we got together.

"Once we started having each other there wasn't no such a thing as too much. We was doing it in Silk's car. We was doing it in the park. We even drove out to Morris Plains one night and snuck and did it in one of them rich people's swimming pools. I swear to God we did. One night when his car broke down we got the bus to New York and did it in the back of the Greyhound. We did it standing up and every kind of way. Silk was still living with his mother, and he couldn't bring no women round there because she was so in love with him herself she would snap out anytime she saw her baby with a girl. I think in her mind, Silk was still about nine years old. We used to go over to Daddy's house and break into the basement, and that was the first place me and Silk had together. By then, I had missed so much school that I was kicked out anyway. I guess you had a good idea what I was doing, and I liked the way you never dogged me. I guess you figured I had been through enough to know what the hell I was doing, but I still didn't want to tell you I was expelled from school until I had gone ahead and quit and had a job, so you could see I could take care of myself.

"We set up house down in the basement of Twenty-eight, but we aint use it all that much really, because I didn't want my father to find us down there. I couldn't have gone through that. Silk built us a bed with a board, some cinder blocks and a mattress he found. We burned candles down there for light and kept boards at the windows. He fixed a radio that was down there, and we used to play it real low late at night. I never told him nothing about how Daddy had busted my cherry when I wasn't but eleven, but Silk used to tell me I could sure fuck to be only in high school. I just said, well, I had done it with an older man once, and that was where we left it. I used to pull out those trunks and things that belonged to Mozelle, though, and fix myself with headdresses and beads for Silk to have me the same way Daddy did. Silk found some of Daddy's old trunks filled with suits from the fifties and forties. Some of those suits was packed away in mothballs, and Silk went crazy over those clothes. There was all kinds of hats that fitted him to a tee, double-breasted jackets with the four-pointed handkerchiefs in the pocket, big pleated trousers that he loved, silk shirts and socks, ties, and a white tuxedo he started wearing when he had that first band of his: Living Blues. He even found a gold-plated trumpet down there with ivory keys in a box lined with satin.

"It was by me and Silk hunting around there that we come on them gator-skin satchels, the ones you figured was so full of gold. We almost blew our cover down there the night Silk found those bags tucked in an opening in the wall that was sealed off with a plank. 'Shheee-it!' he screamed before he knew it, and when I got over to where he was at, he told me, 'Baby, we rich for real.' We started dancing and carrying on, acting like fools. 'Your father must have been something else,' Silk said. 'He was a man all right,' I said. We stayed up planning about what we was going to do with the money we could get for that gold. We wasn't going to take it all, just three of those bags would make us rich, Silk said. It was his idea to leave the other two sealed in there where we found them. He figured that the kind of man my father must have been, we ought to just leave it down there for him, and we would seal it up for him more better, whether Daddy even remembered it was down there any-more or even cared anything about it. Just out of respect. So we brung our three satchels out to our bed. We sealed the other two in the wall good, and Silk made it so nobody wouldn't be able to find them even if they was looking for them.

"Then we sat on the bed smoking and talking about all the things we would do with that money. We was going to have us a couple of houses and some cars. We was going to wait till it got zero cold in Newark, then we was going down to Jamaica and lay in the sunshine long as we wanted to, smoking herb and swimming. Silk was going to finish his music degree at Columbia. We was going to travel to Africa so Silk could learn more about the roots of his kind of music. We was going to Paris to live for a while because Silk said the French people really dig jazz. I couldn't think up all that much I wanted to do with the money myself, so I just listened to Silk mostly. I only wanted the money because it would make it more easy for me and Silk to be together and get married and have a decent life.

"Right before it got light, me and him took our satchels out the basement and put them in Silk's car. He said we couldn't just show up at a bank with all that gold or they would think these niggers done stole this shit. So we snuck into his mother's house and hid most of it in her cellar. We took two bricks with us, then we went downtown and hung out till the banks opened. I went to Prudential and Silk went to First National. We both was using the same story. This piece of gold was what belonged to our grandfather, and we wanted to get it changed into cash money, and yes we wanted to open an account with the bank.

"After we went to the banks we was supposed to meet at Nathan's and celebrate with hot dogs and orange drinks. We both got to that hot-dog stand with the same damn story. It turned out we aint have no gold. What we had is what they call gold brick. It aint nothing but a cheap metal gilded over to look like gold. The woman that saw me at Prudential said it wasn't nothing but a substitute for gold.

"That was the damn fortune in gold you saw my father bring with him when he got back from Europe in '63. If he had those satchels, like you say, in '63, he must have been using them for a grandstand, because none of that 'gold' wasn't worth nothing.

"Still, after that, me and Silk went right ahead after some of those same dreams we talked about the night we found the satchels. Silk said he was going to marry me. He kept talking about quitting his courses for court stenographing at Rutgers so he could get a full-time job that would pay better than his uncle's candy store. Then we was going to move to New York, baby, and get a place in the Village. Silk was applying for a scholarship at Columbia, he said, though I didn't never see no application. We was getting married as soon as he got his Columbia music degree. We would live in the Village. Silk would gig with jazz bands, get the connections he needed so he could pick up some studio work, teach here and there, eventually get his own band together—the whole trip. I don't know what I was planning on doing exactly besides being with Silk—work in a restaurant I guess. I hadn't thought about no babies yet.

"Working in a restaurant was just what I was doing when we got our first apartment across from Weequahic Park. Plus I was the one paying the rent most of the time. I was waitressing at this family restaurant in Montclair. Silk's uncle got me that job. I had to lie about my age. Damn if I didn't look like I was about thirty anyway. It was a good job. The money wasn't bad. I was bringing home twenty, thirty dollars most nights with tips. I was working hard too.

"Daddy wasn't sick then. He had some old chippy living with him spending her Social Security checks for wine and cigars.

"Me and Silk had that apartment. It was freaked off. We had a stereo, color television, push-button phones, satin drapes. I figured I was off the Hill at last doing my thing, but I used to wish sometime Daddy or you could have come by and just sat and talked, you know, seen me in somewhere decent. We had Mediterranean furniture with those big lamps with the heavy chains to turn on the bulbs. It was in that apartment where I first really started to dig jazz. We would sit around, high off Champale, sucking reefers, listening to records and watching TV with the sound off. Silk had all his records there he had moved out of his mother's house. He must have had about three hundred records. I was digging Lady Day and Miss Sassy. When I heard Dinah Washington sing 'Evil Gal Blues' I wore that record out. I even dug songs without no words. I dug 'Straight, No Chaser' and

'This Time the Dream's on Me.' Mornings be rising hot and tropic inside Silk's saxophone. Silk be in the kitchen running scales or breaking down a solo. I be in the bathroom laying in a tub full of milk. By time I'm dressed and in the kitchen, Silk have a pot of herb tea on the table. Then he get the whole stove going with balm-wrapped fish, asparagus, corn tortillas, grits, gravy, cherry pancakes, fresh-grind coffee with lemon rind—all kind of food. Silk was the real cook. We used to go all over—even New York—to get all his exotic food and spices. We was using spices on our skin—like the paste Silk used to make out of turmeric and milk. We was conditioning our hair with mashed avocados. We even brought food into our sex, improvising, licking lemon and mango juice off each other, rubbing one another with walnut oil and peanut oil. Nights was cooled out and magic: Silk wearing his big white bathrobe with purple birds flying in it. Silk sucking on a piece of ginseng root. Me with my eyes lined with kohl and my hips wrapped in red cloth. Laying each other out on the carpet. The music and reefer taking us, till we wasn't in Newark no more and had moved inside each other, Silk holding on, while I rocked us further and further out.

"Everything was cool. I wish you could have seen me in my act. The only problem was it aint last. Silk was still going to school studying his court-stenographing shit, even though he didn't want to be a court stenographer no more. I didn't know then about his police record. He still had his red and black Trans Am, still had his part-time job at his uncle's store where he was selling ten-dollar sets of heroin and loose joints on the side, but I didn't know about it, because I didn't want to know. Sometime he would be the DJ for the jazz program on the campus radio station. He had put together his first band—Living Blues—and they was always practicing in our place which would work on my goddamn nerves, except at least when they practiced in our crib I knew where the hell he was.

"Like I say, he was selling stuff for his uncle out of that candy store, and I didn't find out about that till later, but as far as I know, up to that point, Silk wasn't messing with that shit himself. He was tipping out on me with his other bitches, though, and I didn't like it. When you live with a man you don't need no girlfriends to tell you where they seen your man or who he was with or any of that shit. I knew there was a dead cat on the line. Plus he started to hitting me behind stupid shit, talking about I didn't keep the place clean and I knew he brought his friends over there, couldn't I keep myself no better than that, why was my hair always standing up all over my head and old evil mess like that there. He would wake up sometime ready to kick my ass if he *dreamed* I was pregnant and might have to quit my job. And I was a dumb enough dog to still be in love with him, because if he *was* already taking that dope, it wasn't making him look no uglier. I was in love with that nigger from his process down to his toes. I loved the way the nigger ragged. He could wear some boss vines. He had a long military coat with epaulets and gold braids, white sequin socks and naval Oxfords. He had that tiny star and crescent he used to wear in his ear. Silk got hair over his whole body. He got a real nice chest and arms. I used to love to feel his fine chest hairs brushing my breasts when we made love.

"I still had to go ahead and quit my job at the restaurant because the owner was all the time on my nerves. One night I had seven tables in my station, and she come giving me a lot of noise about my white shoes not being clean. I was so goddamn mad. Them other girls would play up to her. I wouldn't. That's why she was always on me the hardest. I whipped off those shoes and threw them at her. In the middle of her restaurant. If I'm lying, I'm flying. I swear before God. I told her she could take those white shoes and stick them in her white ass. I walked out of there and took the bus home barefoot that night. And then I have to twist the key in my door and walk in on Silk laying up in *my* bed screwing this Puerto Rican drag bitch that lived in our building called herself Miss Fred. By then, Silk was liable to be fucking anything for money so he could get that shit he was using to stick in his arms four and five times a day. He wasn't working nowhere. The dudes he was playing in the band with put his ass out because he wasn't reliable. He had stole so much shit out of his mother's house she had the police looking for him.

"He was still holding down his course at Rutgers some kind of way. Don't ask me how. Anybody could have seen his court stenographer idea wasn't going to get him nowhere, but I think with Silk it meant the only security he had. He used to come home and open up his leather briefcase and lay all his papers out on the bed and sit there, all high, acting like he was studying legal shit. He wasn't putting on no act for me. Silk was psyching out his own self.

"I was still trying to stick with him, thinking I could help him make something out of himself. I looked in the paper and got this job I got now working out in Belleville for this family. I'm out there scrubbing floors, washing and ironing, while he was all doped up, might be anywhere or liable to be waiting for me at the door when I got home to kick my ass, telling me I got another lover, or that I'm doing it with white boys out in Belleville. Then one day he was getting dressed in his mohair suit, getting ready to go out, and I said, 'Silk, please don't go out tonight. You aint headed for nothing but trouble. Why don't you stay here with me.' He didn't look like he even listened. He went in the chifforobe and got my pocketbook. He took out my cigarettes and all the money I had—my week's pay after I made my bank deposit. It was about seventy dollars. He stopped and looked at me on his way out. 'Bitch, what you mean?' he said. He jammed the cigarettes and the seventy dollars in his pants. 'Stay here with you? Shit. I just took everything you got that I want.' I didn't feel like saying nothing. It wasn't nothing but his dope talking. So I said (I was already on the bed in my half-slip), 'Come on, baby, take off those clothes and get in the bed. Get in the bed and get your nut. Then we can take a hot bath.' He looked at me. 'Maybe that shit worked on your father, but I aint interested, bitch.'

"And that was too much for me. I watched Silk walk out of there and I knew I was letting him walk out that time for real. I don't know when he came back and tried his key in the door, because I had moved out. I put all his boss clothes—ripped up—one by one down the shaft to the incinerator. I pawned his stereo, his records. I told the landlord to do what he wanted with the furniture. I didn't want it. The family I work for let me stay with them for a while. I told them I broke up with my boyfriend. They said I'm a good worker, so they aint mind me staying up there. They was glad to get me full-time long as I needed a place to live, but I aint like living out there. I was working for them, plus I would go and work for other families in the neighborhood. I aint do nothing but work.

"I didn't know I was pregnant till I was five months. That was when the baby started to move. I kept working right up till I began to show. Then I came back on the Hill with the money I saved and got a sleeping room till it was time for me to go in the hospital. When Man was born, I found out how to get on welfare. My social worker got me an apartment in the Hayes Projects, which wasn't no big damn favor, because that place aint nothing but a prison without guards. Me and Silk made up. He wasn't using dope. He was in an electronics course at Rutgers. He got a taxicab to drive. He wasn't playing his music no more. I had some good birth control from the Planned Parenthood clinic, and I found out how to use it. We aint stay together no time, though. I couldn't deal with knowing he knew about me and my father, even though we aint talk about it. I couldn't stand Silk knowing about it. That's the reason why I never told him, but somebody did or he just figured it out.

"We aint have no fight or nothing. I just got more and more evil. He aint come home one day. Then I aint see him no more. Somebody said he had got caught with some other boys trying to rob a cleaning store and that he was in Yardville Youth Correction Center. I thought he might call me or write, but he never did. Somebody else said they seen him down at Rutgers with his books. So I just aint know what to think. Once he was gone I couldn't hardly make it on my welfare check. I had started going around to see Daddy every once in a while after Man was born, letting him see his grandchild.

"Daddy got real sick along about February. Around there sometime, after I moved back in Twenty-eight, was when I got hooked back up with you.

"It worked out that I was getting a little bit more money in my check and more food stamps for taking care of Daddy, but he was so sick, and by me spending all I had trying to take care of him, I wasn't making no kind of headway. So I got in touch with the same people I work for in Belleville. They said they had a girl cleaning and cooking for them but she aint work out, so I could have my job back. I figured, hell, I'm just going to risk my social worker finding out I'm working. I got a baby-sitter and went on back to work. I borrowed about six hundred dollars altogether from the family I work for to get electric and telephone service started back up in that house and clearing Daddy's old bills—money I'm still paying off in installments out of my paycheck. I'm just making it the best way I know how, Sister. I aint going to lay down and die. Shit. I'm going for me *and* a baby. I aint letting my father die neither, I'll tell you that.

"I can't turn from my father. I can't even hate Silk no more really. Even though, like I say, I don't need Silk, and if he was here right now I would probably curse him out, I loved hell out of that nigger once. He turn me on to the only music can speak to me even now. Plus he still the father of my baby."

6.

"I'm going to build me a Heaven,
have a Kingdom of my own [twice]
Where these brownskin women
can cluster round my throne"

—BLUES

~~~ *P*oole opened his eyes. He was not dead. He could hear the birds behind the house whistling inside the trees. He sensed the night at his blinds twisting over the world like an incense.

The room was there yet vanished, lit by his soul's abiding memories: the close, high-walled room full of shadows and plants. He came to himself. His hands moved down to feel the running sores at his groin and legs. He burned and froze in turns. His head ached.

He began to float again. Out of the reach of pain. Past the room and the streets full of houses and trees.

A flash of lightning moved across the clouds. It was only a moment, and then the preacher had him upright in the water blessing him with the Holy Ghost. There was another flash of lightning. Then the rain beat heavily into the swamplands. The old women were leaving the rocks. The other children swam the thundering space to land. He turned, but the preacher had fastened on to his arm.

"God aint give us the spirit of fear," the preacher said. "Fear is from the Devil, boy."

The preacher's voice rang in the middle of the water.

He was transfixed, wedded to that voice:

". . . the lightning that gave birth to you, boy, the coming together of mother and father."

"Don't nobody know nothing about his father. They give him the name Sam at the orphanage, and I baptized him. The orphanage baptizes all our children early. His mother come around to see him a few times, but she aint want nothing to do with him except 'Is he all right?' and 'Here a few dollars.' She been in and out of jails so much she aint fit to raise a child under law no how. Pretty yellow gal, too—almost pass for white. Mozelle, her name is. I hear tell she killed a negro she was going with and didn't do no time for that. She mess with them Italian men in the French Quarter. One of them Sicilians got her set up in a fancy house what don't service nothing but rich white men what likes light-skin colored gals. Aint a black man allowed in there except for the little boys she got serving drinks. Even the piano players is all mulattoes.

"Anyway, 'Sieur, you don't want to hear about the sinful woman. She aint been to see after the boy in two, three years. Done lost interest, I guess. She aint living no kind of life. I hear tell she dances naked with the voodoos on Congo Square. Fine white ladies comes to them dances and lays down on the ground and roll on they bellies. So I hear tell, 'Sieur.

"Anyway, we just glad to place the boy in a good home with a man of refinement what can make something out of him."

The huge stranger picked up the boy and held him in his arms. They were in the orphanage minister's dark office. The two old men stood together, smiling at the gold-skinned boy.

"It won't be hard to make something of this one," said Old Sylva, holding the boy's long, pale hands. "He's fine. Looks like one of my own children. Fine boy. I've been married twice—two good women—and have no son to leave after me. Norbert got killed in war. I'm going to raise this one so people will swear his pedigree reaches back to God Himself."

His mind opened like a bright fan. He ran hard and fast. He felt the wind inside him, pulling him through the tangled woods. He ran out into the glittering sunlight. He came to rest beside the swamp. He crouched and touched the ground, waiting for the silence to wash him like a rush light. He was married to that stillness. Married to the place with emerald water that gave off a spectral illumination. He was married to the pure, sweet water and rootless ground. The deep, siren sighs of the swamp called his secret name. The sunfish and egrets, the cypress, and the grasshoppers, big as a grown person's finger, the Spanish moss, the mullein plants, the snakes and cotton mice—all knew his name. The rattling palmettoes called him.

He pushed his hair from his face and lay on the ground. For comfort's sake, he removed his shoes and stretched his legs. He could relax his whole body. There was no one to correct him now or appraise him like a thing set up in a shop to be sold. That was how it was at the school he attended for mulatto children.

"If you're not careful, boy," the schoolteacher, Mrs. Hemecourt, always told him, "you'll never amount to anything. You're *lucky* enough—lucky as Moses rolling through the bullrushes, but what do you aim to do with all that good fortune?"

His luck, he knew, lay in old Dominick Sylva, the richest colored man in New Orleans, having taken him in to raise him like his own son. Old Sylva, as he was called even by the white people and men his own age, had made his fortune in real estate and slaves. He was mean and wise enough to do what he *had* to do, buying and selling negroes in Charleston and New Orleans until the war. Sylva walked the world in big, fierce strides. The blood of three people ran through his veins: French, Spanish and African; though nothing in his appearance bespoke the drop of black blood linking him to the tropic race. Could have passed for a pure Creole if not for the public record in the city archives office. His father had been a white man from Bordeaux, his mother an octoroon.

He loved the boy. Old Sylva hunted and fished with him and called him pet names like "Shimmer" and "Firefly."

Sylva had had a daughter who died during an epidemic of yellow fever that came in one terrible heat of summer. After grueling treatments of mercurial purges, blankets and alkali washes, the child died, bled white by leeches meant to "draw out humors."

"You look just like that child," Zozo said to him once. "Could have been your twin sister. Same hard black eyes and bright skin. Hold your mouth like her too, like you sucking down the cool starlight. You about the same age she was when she left this world, poor soul. I don't reckon she had more than seven years. You is sure a pretty boy, the God's truth be told. Come on here and help Aunt Zozo tote these clothes back to the great house, and I'll let you have chocolate."

"Too pretty for your own good." That would be Mrs. Hemecourt when he failed to prepare his lessons. Her spectacles would be shining like a double sun. Something in her voice would tell him that she was genuinely afraid for him. "Be better off if you were black as anybody's negro on the Congo with corn-hard hands. This white man's world isn't what it was: Since the Reconstruction, a mob would just as soon string you up as a pure nigger out of a cotton field. You have to take hold of education, son, like it were gold. You have to start now to put foolishness from your mind, if you want to last!"

He already knew he would last. He was going to be a great

man, greater than any man in Louisiana—colored or white. Old Sylva had decreed it.

"You have to let these women fret over you the way they do. They don't mean no harm."

He was good at spelling and counting. He could read children's stories printed in English and French. Mother Elodie, the second Mrs. Sylva, had engaged a straight-haired colored man to teach him to play the piano. He practiced Czerny's five-finger exercises, and once he played *Twinkle, Twinkle, Little Star* at a church recital sponsored by one of Mother Elodie's ladies societies. The ivory-, yellow-, and cherry-tinted ladies asked him if he wanted to grow up to study in Europe and become a famous concert pianist. He said he might. He did not know anything about Europe. He had a pony named Africa. He told the church women he liked it when Africa jumped.

Old Sylva had the boy's name changed to Gabriel. He guessed Gabriel was a good name for himself but had liked Sam fine. All the other boys at school had names like Nicolas, Camille, and Antoine. Maybe Sam was not a good name. Old Sylva knew what was best.

He turned over on his back and looked up at the sky. Bobwhites were calling over a field far away. Today he would miss the whole school day, lying here. Mrs. Hemecourt would call on his papa this evening. Old Sylva would laugh as soon as she was gone, mincing his lips and imitating her straight stance and high voice.

Then Mother Elodie would say that was no example for the boy, and Zozo would call them into the dining room for supper.

"Almighty and gracious God, make us grateful for what we are about to receive . . ."

He *was* lucky. He had Sylva to dote on him. He had the love of Mother Elodie and Zozo. The straight-haired piano teacher called him his best young pupil. Even Mrs. Hemecourt was fond of him in her own way.

Still, sometimes, his mood grew black. Then he would come to the swamp. The black, heartsore mood always began when he thought of his mother. He missed her. Though he did not have a tangible memory of her, he felt her present in the swamp. The swamp confirmed her. The swamp, like the mother who came to him in his dreams, was full, fragrant and cool. She would not be aging and stiff-mouthed like Mother Elodie or Zozo. She was beautiful and young. He dreamed of her often—a mother, sister, bride—and when he did, he would awake crying and unable to stop.

Elijah's chariot stopped by this house Friday evening. Through the eyes of faith he saw the chariot—Elijah's chariot—rocking in the middle of the air.

The hot night embraced him. From his bed he watched the treelined courtyard. He hated the dark, and nights took so long to get through. He slept lightly. Mother Elodie forbade him to leave the lamp burning in the room. Even when he managed to doze off, the slightest sound woke him: the crickets' ringing, the whir of leaves, shutters rattling a downstairs window. Then he sat, at the very edge of the bed, waiting for morning, watching weaving shadows in the courtyard, sensing something out there sinister and secret.

The Devil was out there. He knew. The Devil had walked up out the Mississippi, an army of brutes dragging behind him. On the large bed he listened, afraid of the sound of his own breathing.

Sleep on, soul. Sleep in Jesus.

His body relaxed when he heard the milkman's wagon moving in unison with the wind. He lay back. His soft bed, and the pillows filled with peach leaves and verbena, soothed him like a mother. He stretched his fingers to tease the air. The smells of river moss and magnolias rushed up into the room. The birds began to whistle cautiously. Then the first light struck the trees.

Let our souls say, amen. Death is a dictator no man escapes.
Amen.

The voices of the visitors downstairs traveled the house. The voices began slowly and resolutely to sing:

One glad morning, when this life is over, I'll fly away.

Soon there would be the funeral. They were going to put Old Sylva inside a tomb. Relatives and friends had remained awake all night downstairs with the body, talking and praying and singing. Zozo said they did that to protect a person's soul from evil while passing from this world into the next.

Hallelujah! Hallelujah, by and by, I'll fly away.

The door to his room opened and Zozo entered, a frail, black woman in a brilliant tignon. She limped over to the bed, carrying a basin and pitcher. A yellow towel was tossed over her shoulder. One of her legs was slightly shorter than the other. She steadied herself on that shortest leg and lifted him from the bed. He was always awed by her strength.

Her toothless grin was somewhere between a baby's and a hag's. No one knew for certain how old Zozo was. She had been Sylva's nurse when he was a boy, had bathed and dressed him until he was eight years old.

"How did you sleep?" she asked him.

"I *never* sleep. I've told you," he complained softly.

"Everybody sleep," said Zozo, "or they die." She took his chin in her hand and turned his face playfully from side to side. "I reckon you slept enough to last the day."

She laid the basin on the nightstand.

He raised his arms for her to pull his nightshirt over his head.

"The Devil was out there," he told her, "inside the courtyard. I saw his tail slide back behind one of the trees."

He watched her put away his nightshirt in the hamper. He flipped his short penis up and down.

Zozo came and slapped his hands. "You too full of talk about the Devil for your own good." She washed him in the lemon-scented water.

"Ou est Maman Elodie?"

Zozo brought his white shirt and white suit from the wardrobe. Yesterday, he had watched her stir the shirt in boiling water. Then she turned it through the wringer and hung it in the sun behind the kitchen. Now, the boiled, rough-dry shirt was starched and dazzling, flying toward him on a hanger in Zozo's hand.

She went in her apron pocket and handed him a pair of socks. He put them on.

"Mam'selle Elodie downstairs with company."

"Where is Père Sylva?"

"Laid out down there in the parlor. Now, put your legs in these pants and don't ask me no more questions, hear?"

"I have to go look at him?"

"Sure, you must look at him. You have seven. That's old enough to pay respect to the dead."

"I won't."

"You have to view the body, child. What got into you? Don't you love Old Sylva no more? He wouldn't want to leave this world without his crest jewel saying good-bye."

"I don't want to say good-bye," he told her, and struck the side of his leg like a general. "If he loved me, he wouldn't've died. I won't die!"

"Lord," said Zozo, brushing brilliantine through his hair, "you just like him for the world."

He walked into the relative coolness of the parlor. He saw Mother Elodie coming to him from the other end of the carpet. She wore a long berry-black dress. A black handkerchief floated at her waist, fastened there by a cluster of diamonds. She took his hand.

"Come," she said, forcing a smile. "Let us pay respects to Père Sylva. *Allons-y, mon enfant.*"

She lay her hand behind his head. Her smell always reminded him of the lemon-scented water he was bathed in. She held him close to the skirt of her dress. He glimpsed Sylva's body lying on a table in front of the beveled-glass doors surrounded by baskets of goldenrods. He became aware of the guests in the room sitting, drinking coffee. It occurred to him that they might be drinking café au lait with chocolate, and if he was well behaved, Zozo might let him have some. The guests watched him. There was Mr. Paris, the cigar maker, as usual hugging his fat belly; the Widow Rhett; Pastor and Mrs. Thompson; and Pastor Thompson's mother, who people said kept the lamp burning in her bedroom at night though she was blind. These were Sylva's oldest friends. They were the finest of the black Creole families left in New Orleans since the war. He hated to misbehave in front of them. It would not please Sylva, he knew, him protesting, crying like a baby before these people, afraid to look at a dead body. Sylva abominated any ungentlemanly behavior.

But he did not want to see Sylva rigid, gray from death's heavy touch like the dead birds he sometimes came across while playing in the garden.

"*Allons-y, mon enfant.*"

He wanted to remember him as he had been, crackling with his strong life, walking the world with a ferocious swagger. He wanted to turn and see him step into the foyer the way he had, removing his black, wide-brimmed hat in the same instant and undoing his frock coat. He would run and take the coat, hat and gold-tipped cane and give them to Zozo, then receive the kiss from the center of the white moustache and neat imperial. Sylva had ruled the enchanted kingdom of the boy's childhood. His own life would dry to dust and blow away without Sylva's liquid voice bubbling, rising and falling on him.

He pulled away from Mother Elodie and began to run. Paris, the squat cigar maker, intercepted him by the door. Mr. Paris smelled of yellow tobacco and oil of Makassar and the cheap women he visited on Perdido Street.

He fought, but the ugly little man held on to him. He broke the pearl buttons on his shirt, struggling. One moment he was kicking and shouting, upsetting furniture, clawing the air, and the next moment, as though he vanished through rage and returned cleansed to the room, he lay calmly on his back, with Mr. Paris's soft sweating hands on his chest.

Mother Elodie stood vertically over him, fanning him with a luminous fan made of peacock feathers.

She bent down and spoke to him in a voice that was new and hard to his ears. "What man shall not see death?" she asked. "But thanks be to God: We are cast down, but not destroyed. We are delivered to death for Jesus' sake that the life of Jesus might be made manifest in our body." Her mouth worked so slowly it seemed not to move at all. "Don't be afraid, boy."

He went with her now, his shirt bunched in the front, to where Sylva lay in chilling grandeur, eyes shut, stiff and blanched. He watched her remove the wedding band from Sylva's finger. She placed the ring in his tiny hand. "Now this is yours," she told him.

He grasped the ring so tightly it made an imprint in the center of his palm.

He was in the dining room with the other children—gold-skinned boys and girls with black curling hair and fine, high-bridged noses. They sat together staring like a nest of golden kittens.

The table was in front of them covered with the feast. Roasted partridge, swan, calf livers, catfish and bass were displayed on trays. In silver bowls yam fritters had been set with rice-meal balls, fried biscuits and twice-fried plantains and grits cooked with grease and pieces of venison. Bowls of okra gumbo were laid on the sideboards by the window.

Past the table, the parlor was filled with wavering light. Three candelabra, each containing six candles, blazed on top of the table where Sylva's body had lain.

A woman stood inside the parlor, singing a spiritual—a slow, black moaning to God. The singer was an ex-slave who rocked to the rhythm of her song with a sensual, fleshy movement, her head flung back, her hands now open, now tightly shut at her sides.

Through the dining-room windows he saw the other negroes who had come to say good-bye to Sylva, the men with shimmering black bodies naked to the waist, the women wearing head ties and slack dresses. They had been at the cemetery this afternoon, standing a distance away from the other mourners, shaded by oak trees and gray-green garlands of moss, giving the same respect they afforded whites. Now they listened to the song rolling from the house. The world was listening.

> *If you never hear me sing no more*
> *Aw, meet me on the other shore,*
> *God's gonna separate the wheat from the tares,*
> *Didn't he say?*

He looked at the singer again, as if to understand her. There she stood, gross-lipped and heavy-haunched, singing a song that came down to her through her blood. His own blood, Sylva taught him, was different from the blood of common negroes. His natural father was no doubt a white man, like Sylva's. It was said of his mother that she was the color of yellow jade.

"The blood of the pure blacks will never be equal to ours," Sylva had said, "no matter what Emancipation tried to do to disgrace the great *gens de couleur libres* and place us on the same footing as ex-slaves. I owned a hundred slaves. My people were bred for luxury, bred to be as good as the white man, with his own blood. Our women are the most beautiful women in the South, exotic plants produced in a force bed, produced only for love—love higher than any white woman or any iron-black woman knows.

"Mother Elodie's father was from Santo Domingo—a quadroon, who fought in the Battle of New Orleans. We are no Africans, descended from an unknown black beast. A nigger, boy, is the worst thing in the world. Never let anyone put you in their class. The South was built on the classes of men: white, yellow and black. Destroy the classes, and the South will be destroyed."

He had not questioned Sylva's teachings. What Old Sylva knew he had learned through living out of times long before the boy's birth and from serious books which he studied when the house was still and everyone else was asleep.

Yet when he looked at this black, bovine, God-moaning woman standing before Mother Elodie and the colored Creoles in the parlor, he failed to see an inferior, a descendant of a beast. What he saw, sitting in the spell of her song, though he could not have called her this, was a mystical mother-father, the human-god-beast in one, singing with the same cello-rich authority Sylva used when he spoke. He saw a power equal to the majesty and peace and dignity his beloved Sylva had had.

Then her song ended, while he was climbing up into it, weightless in time. She was leaving the house, her voice still ringing in the background. Mother Elodie stood by the door, speaking to the back of that beaver-brown woman. The house guests also stood, their habitually depthless faces transformed.

Dusk had begun. The negroes outside had turned into gleam-eyed spirits. The birds whistled in reverse.

Another stranger came into the house, a woman wearing a looped-up red gown. Her hair, like a whipped black plume, framed her face and shoulders. Her eyes saw him the moment she entered the house. Mother Elodie and the guests stepped back, mesmerized, to let the woman pass, forming a clear lane from the door to the dining room.

The gown made a swishing noise as she moved. He watched her. The heels of her shoes clicked with clocklike deliberation, sending a soft rumbling through the floorboards and through his chest.

She came around the feast table. The other children beside him began to whimper. She spread her palms wide and they ceased, gazing quiet and caught.

With excruciating attention her hand lingered on his curling hair. He smelled jasmine on her, magnolia and oleander. She touched his forehead, and he felt her immaculate coolness.

"What is your name?" she rasped.

He could not resist her, and he *knew*. "Sam," he said, surprised by his own voice.

"I'm your mother, baby." Her earbells tinkled in time to her slow, saucy speech. "You don't ever need to be without Mozelle again."

She touched the edges of his face and gave a long, carnal sigh. "You going to grow up to be a sweet," she said. "Women is always going to be in love with you, and you never going to work no regular job. You going to make a fortune not only for yourself but for generations on into the fourth generation. Only God can bless the fourth generation. Says so right in the Bible, but you going to be able to do even that."

It was not a dream. She had been in this house. She had claimed him. Her touch had turned something inside him, like a river grabbing the land in rich overflow, washing away all responsibility and time and sense. He stood up in his bed, burning with fever, delirious with visions of the cool immaculate mother.

"Maman!" He screamed for the pure pain and pleasure of wrenching his soul.

Zozo came in and tried to lay him down.

He stiffened. His hands turned white gripping the bedpost. His nightshirt was soaked with urine and sweat. For three nights running the child had awaken at the precise middle of night, screaming for Mozelle.

Mother Elodie ran into the room, in her dressing jacket and boudoir cap.

Zozo had been feeding him chamomile tea for three days with no benefit. The doctor who came to look at the child suggested a bath in cracked ice, but Mother Elodie was afraid, so Zozo had been set to her own doctoring.

Mother Elodie was speaking, standing by the window. "It's the evil she brought into my house, the horned viper, coming in here with her cheap clothes, without a drop of respect for the dead. She wouldn't have dared step near this place if he was still living. She must think because of the life she lives she can do as she pleases, terrorizing that poor child, parading in here like a queen. If she comes back, I'll put the law on her: God is my witness."

Zozo had him down on the bed now, rubbing his back with dried leaves. "Nothing you can do with that Devil-woman, Mam'selle. Aint you seen how she had the peoples hypnotized when she come in here? She running that hook crib down the Quarter and you think the police pays it a bit of mind? You think she fears police? She has police in her pay. That woman no got the fear of God or man in her."

"She fears death if she's human. Let her come back here. . . . I'll take Mr. Sylva's gun and kill her."

Sleep careened through his body, carrying his mind past voices, house and sky. He struggled to remain conscious, but the deft rustling of leaves at his back did its work. He was moving through a crystalline river of thoughtfreeness, a swirling white river of cleansing, moving through him, cleaning away sorrow, darkness and fear.

He awoke to the full glare of morning. Zozo and Mother Elodie were speaking in the hall.

He heard Zozo's thin voice declare, "She still the boy's mother."

"And what kind of mother?" The question was a sudden burr, sailing the air. "She gave away her right to mothering when he was an infant so she could run with her men. Who knows the number of babies she has laid down and birthed, then got up from, like a beast, leaving them to their daddies or some workhouse? What do you think she came here for? She doesn't want that boy. She came here to raise the Devil. That's what she came for.

"That girl is a shame before God. I hate to think what would have become of Gabriel—Sam is no fit name for him—if Old Sylva hadn't swallowed pride and principle both and went to the orphanage and brought him here.

"I always loved children. I never had any of my own. I promised Jesus the night Gabriel first came into this house to take the boy and rear him above the recklessness of his mother. I promised that. I won't go back on it."

"This got nothing to do with promises made with God. I love the boy good as you, Mam'selle. I still say, whatever she is, she is his mother. The picking of what mother to bring this or that soul into the world is a mystery we can't understand. She did him no harm. His fever broke right along before morning. He have too much excitement is all. She did no harm coming and leaving the way she done. This is the house of her father. She the only child Sylva have left. The boy die in the war. The other girl ripped from life when she was a little thing by the fever. Sylva tell everybody *she* die too, and I back him up twenty years, but we know she come back to New Orleans and call herself Mozelle."

She never came back, though he waited, went to the swamp less and less, secretly hoping she would come and cast her spell on the house again.

It was Zozo who finally told him about his mother, one spring night when he was nine years old. They were inside Zozo's cabin behind the yard of the main house. The walls were papered with newsprint. There was a thin fire in the hearth before which she sat, her lined black face tinted with red.

"The people said it was your mother put the first Mrs. Sylva down in her grave, when she was twenty-six, grieving over her child. Your mother was born with pupils in her eyes shaped like half-moons. I know because I midwifed her. She was pretty as a little cupid. *Everything* on her was fine. She always had a strong will. She loved the moon too much. From the time she knew how to talk and ask for what she want, she'd sit in her bed at night, looking out the window, crying till her eyes was swole, begging for the moon. We wasn't able to satisfy her. One night, Old Sylva took a notion to hold a mirror to the window so it caught the moon's reflection. Then he put the mirror in her little hands. That used to content her. He loved that child and would have pulled down the moon-self if it was in his power. She come down with fever the same as the other baby girl did—they was ten months apart—but she lived, and I believe it was because her will was stronger, and, little as she was, she was feeding off that other baby's life.

"She ran away from here when she was thirteen—to lay up with gamblers and murderers. I used to think Old Sylva's heart had to be made out of rock not to break in a hundred pieces over that girl.

"She was doing all manner of sin, pleasuring herself like the carnal night had no morning. We heard she moved up North. We heard she was in jail, and we heard she was dead."

Zozo leaned to the edge of her broken chair. The borderline between the one-room cabin and the night was gossamer.

"It was ten years, then she come back, not to her father's house, but to the French Quarter. One of the crime-rich Italian men had her, covering her down with jewels like a zombie doll. Moved her into a tumbling big house on St. Peter Street."

"All the negro servants goes to her. Even white people goes to her. Say she stronger than God, gets her power from the Devil himself, say: She give spells and charms to do evil and good. They calls her the 'Mother of Whores,' 'Queen of Queens,' 'Consort to Snakes and Crocodiles.'"

"It is time to get right with God," he told the congregation, passion riding each syllable. "We are living in the last days. There won't be any more days like these. It won't be long before everyone will understand what must be done, but it will be too late. It is praying time. If we ever needed prayer, we need it today. If we ever needed the Lord, we need Him today. The tenth chapter, first verse of Ecclesiastes tells us dead flies will cause the apothecary's ointment to send forth a stinking savor. I would have you know today there are dead flies in the church. We have people sitting right in this church, raised in the church and rocked on holy knees, but they're still unclean, because they *still* need to be washed in the blood of the crucified Christ."

The words swirled over the church, failing to fuse the spirit of the congregation. The congregation of Holy Love Methodist Church looked on the pretty-faced preacher as though they did not know him, when in truth most of them had watched him grow into a man. Had been there when Old Sylva was laid to rest in his elaborate tomb and looked into the boy's eyes whose sweeping lashes by rights belonged to a girl. Looked now, waiting for nothing apparently, protected by the armor of their fine clothes and drawn faces. But he knew, by the pained light ebbing in their eyes, that they felt the sting of accusation in his words.

They believed if they could disclaim all recognition of the words, pretend he was not speaking words at all—no words, just sounds—they might escape the guilt they shared that almost cold Sunday morning. All of them shared—though only eleven were inside the church on the night the nigger came running and bleeding with terror-fraught shouts down Love Street, chased by a mob of white men. Those eleven who were pulled by the terror-breathing screams from their church business meeting to the windows, and when they *saw,* began to put out the lights and bolt the doors, acting as if moving under the direction of the blindness of all of them.

That nigger, they later picked off the grapevine, was a black man just nineteen and too full of his manhood, who staggered his way drunk into the white men's barroom on the corner and demanded service. Flashed a razor when the virile pushing and clapping and the shouts of "coon boy" and "jigaboo" began. In a quick, air-teasing motion he drew blood from four of the white men. They were laughing until they felt their wounds, none of them cut mortally, but cut all the same. By Sambo. By Rastus. They froze around the purple-lipped nigger. Then, in a sudden flash heat of man's smell, fists, sticks and broken glass, they beat him over the floor. At the door he scrambled, his grizzled hair pouring blood, and began to run through night-empty Love Street, screaming for help.

The wind tore at his ass.

When he came to Holy Love's doors and pounded the smooth wood where the stains of his blood had now soaked in, the hearts of those saints *knew* his cry but could not grasp it. They were silent except for the out-in breathing of listening and waiting while a mob came up on their steps and dragged the nigger away, lynched him, burned him and left his charred body hanging on gibbets in front of the Mississippi River.

"I make this covenant with God," and he snapped his eyes. In a moment he had transcended them. He was swept far at the throne of infinity. He said, "Lord, if you raise me up, I will draw all men—black, yellow, red and white—unto You. Not for form or fashion, Lord, but for the eternal magnification of Your name."

He looked out on the ivory-, yellow- and cherry-tinted faces of this congregation which was not his and which now would never be his. He had been a member of the congregation and a young preacher called by God and so rehearsed in the Word that Pastor Thompson permitted him to preach the sermon on the fourth Sunday of each month. Many in the church said he preached like a Pentecostal circuit rider. Still no one denied his calling or that the Holy Spirit had given him utterance.

He was a pet at Holy Love, indulged for his physical beauty and the music of his voice as well as for the church's reverence of Dominick Sylva's memory. He reembodied Sylva, moving in life with the same ferocious stride as that great dead man. He could do no wrong as far as they were concerned.

Sweat beaded at the bridge of his nose. Wisps of hair clung to his forehead. He stood rigid at the high edge of his destiny from where he could see his past.

These people seated before him were the touchstones of a race, artificial human growths, produced in a lush hothouse. Rare and exotic people of mixed blood. *Sang-mêlé*. Coral-mouthed quadroon. Mulatto. Marabou. Long ago, quadroon balls showcased amber-colored women to a scintillating dusk world. These women, existing at the crossroads of black and white, had "married" white men rich as Croesus and won for themselves and for their night jasmine babies, freedom and wealth, giving birth to a *gens de couleur libres*.

This race of free men of color had been more highly placed than any of their race in the new world. Their men were carpenters, capitalists, architects and lawyers. Their women emulated to the point of surpassing the ease and luxury of white ladies. They lived in houses as big and secure as ships in the Faubourg Marigny. They despised their soot-toned brethren and feared the abolition of slavery, sensing the threat to their own society.

Holy Love Methodist Church was founded in 1851 and had always restricted membership to include only those negroes of wealth and long pedigrees.

Now they were a back-broken people. They had barely survived the war and Reconstruction, and now Jim Crow was sweeping them away forever. The good shining times were over. Jim Crow made little distinction in degree of color or generations of freedom.

"I found out everything I need is in the hand of God."

In the beginning he went to church only to please Mother Elodie. Before long, the idea of salvation obsessed him—salvation not only from sin but from the mysterious evil of Mozelle. While other boys became interested in sports, then girls, then talked of careers and wives, he grew more and more hungry for God. He hungered for a world of piety and justification. He did not smoke or drink. He did not go out with girls, dance or listen to the Devil's music. He studied the Bible, fasted and prayed, asking God to perform a mighty work at Holy Love through the vessel of his life. Now the change had come, and it was *he* who was changed.

Over and over in his mind he saw images of the black man last night outside the tabernacle—like a series of photographs of what he had actually seen and what was easy for him to imagine. The look of . . . what was it? . . . surprise? . . . when the cane cracked under his heart for the seventeenth time, splintering his rib cage. He imagined it was himself out there, his own brains and blood spilling onto the street.

"Sweet Jesus," he had gasped. "We have to help him."

"Hush," a woman whispered, crouched by the window.

Pastor Thompson's slow voice had come seeking him in the

dark: "We got nothing to do with that nigger. You hear me, boy? I'm sorry to say it. Those men wouldn't be after him for no reason. Nigger just like an old dog, always digging up trouble."

He jolted into darkness. "I'm going out there."

Someone hugged him powerfully in the dark.

Pastor Thompson said, "That's right, Brother Bayonne, hold him."

He panted and struggled. Other arms were on him now, restraining him, loving him.

"Hold on to him. If he gets loose he'll go out there and get himself killed. Boy's got to learn how to get by in the world."

They had spent the night inside the church, and when they came out onto the dawn-chilly street, he apologized to the others for his impulsiveness, but he knew he was not the same.

While lying on the church floor he had dreamed the church was shaking, rocking with the world. He ran out into the street. The trees spun their heads and groaned. The sky turned black. He ran toward the lake. When he reached the lake he saw Mozelle, naked, her fierce hair loose, coming up out the water, a blazing candle balanced on top of her head. She stood on the water, full-bodied. She was his mother. He pulled back. A gold diadem lay on the barge by the lake. He reached for the diadem and put it on. Thunderbolts raced to the roof of Heaven. He saw Mozelle smile, her mouth holding the daystar, going back down into the lake.

"I promise to set before God," he said now in the church, "a spirit nation pursuing and exercising *holy love* in deed, word and flesh. To set before Him a regenerated people formed for the King of Heaven. I will do this even if I must make my way in the wilderness and create rivers in the desert. Even," he dared, "if I have to thresh mountains and hills, *I will do this*. I will fan them, and they will be carried away in the wind. I will do a new thing in the spirit. I will work, and who will let it? It will spring from the hand of God."

Pastor Thompson moved up behind him and spoke gently in his ear. "That's enough now, boy. Come on and sit down." The pastor stepped off the pulpit and signaled the organist, who began the lazy strains of "What a Friend We Have in Jesus."

He continued speaking before the stone-faced congregation. His curse rode against the edge of the music: "Lord," he cried, "You are making me tell the truth. The strong-armed and everlasting God is going to strike you down, Holy Love Church. You will be turned back. God will blow on you and wither you away. He will bring you down with your pomp to your grave. The worms will be spread under you and worms will cover you. You will be thrust through with the sword of God and go down to the sides of the pit of Hell."

Mother Elodie was the first to stand, her gloved hand gripping the back of the pew in front of her, rising on one of Sylva's old sword-canes, and walk out of the church.

She was followed by the rest of the congregation, some of them pausing to look back at him and shake their heads.

In the last pew he saw a woman rise like an elegantly unfurling palmetto. She left the church, behind the others. She was Mozelle.

He went to the house eight times before the maid brought him to Mozelle. He walked into a marble foyer, up flights of twisting stairs to the top of the century-old house on St. Peter Street and past a peeling corridor. Her room was filled with mirrors and overflowing with flowers. He entered and lowered his eyes. Mozelle sat in front of a red and black lacquered screen. A large plate of French sweets was set at her feet. She wore only a black lace basque and sheer black gloves. Her opulent breasts overhung the top of her half-cup brassiere. Her eyes flashed behind a lace mask.

"What the hell you want?" she asked him.

He looked up at her. Her nipples were flame-colored on the

brilliantly white body. No one anywhere would have dared to call her a colored woman.

"I've been coming," he stammered. He began again. "I'm your son."

"I know who you are, Preacher."

"I'm your son," he repeated weakly.

"I don't give a damn." Her mouth made a cruel smile that came and went with her talk. "What you want from me? Hey? I watch you come. From there"—she thrust an arm to indicate the round, arched window—"I look and see you pass through Mozelle-gate. Hey? What you need?"

"Do I have to need something to come here to you?"

"The others all need something, no? She is a good house. Make money fast as a steamboat. Ten thousand dollars a week, sometimes more. They come to Mozelle—these rich white sports—when the amusement of family life and the theater fail. I arrange dates for them with my house girls. At first my maid think you were one of them—one of the students who come to Mozelle with rosy faces, rubbing they hat in they hands. I knew who you were the first day you start slowing by the carriageway and searching my window.

"Now you tell me: Why you come to Mozelle? It is long-long before you come to me. So, why?"

His eyes lowered. "I want to know who my father is."

"*Mais,* you can leave that horseshit in the street. You didn't come here to ask me that. You don't have to tell me, *vous savez,* I can tell *you.*" She leaned back in her chair and let go a long breath. "Your father was the Devil." She laughed. "He was more handsome than the Devil. Blond, muscular Frenchman, passing through the gambling rooms one night on Bourbon Street. I used to love the broad-shoulder blondes. He had a beard. Fine clothes. Spoke beautiful French. Gave me three hundred dollars for one night. I spent a week with him. We went to Churchill Downs. He paid fifteen hundred dollars for Mozelle. I didn't ask his name, but he told me anyway. It was Poule, I think. Maybe not. Maybe he wasn't the one."

She stood, cautiously at first, as though she did not trust herself to her feet. She stiffened her back and pulled away her lace mask. Her wide-open eyes were magnificently distant. "Do you think I am not beautiful? I am a woman now more than forty years old and the fresh white boys still talk and dream after me as they did ten, twenty years ago. Your old papa, Père Sylva, was such a fool. He thought girls were only good for embroidery and singing. I," she touched herself lightly, "make more money in and out of season than Père Sylva's miles of cane and cotton. Mozelle is not finished, no?"

She went to the marble-topped dressing table in a corner of the room. He followed her in her mirrors, remarking the cool tempo of her movements. She drew her hair into a chignon at the crown of her head and fastened it.

"Bring the blue dress," Mozelle demanded, lighting a cigar and leaving it to burn in a tray on the table.

There was a rack of dresses behind him. He removed a jet-trimmed gown with puffed up sleeves and deep bretelles over the shoulders. He brought the gown to her.

"Hang it over the screen."

He did so and sat in her chair, resting his face in his broad hands. He looked up when she passed his knees, going behind the screen.

"You still preach?" she asked from behind his head. "That was a good sermon you put to them at Holy Love, yes. You still preach?"

"No, ma'am. I had a little church down on Flood Street, Free Church of the Living God," he told the room, the objects on the dressing table, the huge brass bed covered with mosquito netting. "I was ordained Holiness last winter. We had a small faithful congregation and, praise God, we were growing. Last spring when Big Muddy rose up the way it did, we got washed out down there. I was pastoring to a poor, black fold. There wasn't the money to relocate. I put all I had into that Flood Street tabernacle. I hope to have my own church again soon though. I have to have my own church so I can preach the word the way God directs me.

"I moved out of Père Sylva's house. Mother Elodie . . . well, we don't do anything but argue all the time since what happened at her church. Pastor Thompson wanted to put me on a probation and have the church elders praying for me, but I can't see where I was wrong, and I wouldn't go back on anything I said. I didn't want to be an aggravation to Mother Elodie. She's an old woman. She's not well. Zozo passed away before this last Christmas. Had a stroke standing up in the kitchen. I'm old enough to be on my own. I have a room now not far from here on Toulouse Street."

Mozelle came around the screen and had him fasten the back of her gown. He smelled honey on her, mimosa and lilacs. She went to the dressing table and powdered her breasts with red powder; the top of her dress was bordered with brilliants. She fixed spangled butterflies in her hair.

"You need not to care for it. You a preacher if I ever heard one. You talk before people like you the father of the whole world."

She sat at her table. "Tell Mozelle why you come, dear one."

"Zozo said you give spells to people to perform good or evil. Is that true?"

"They come to me," she told him carefully. "It is the will of the spirit. In one door they come for love and diversion. In another door they come, the disconsolate, for Mozelle-help with their illness and crossed conditions. I work for them at my altar. Perhaps one day you will see. I become a god for them and tell them the tidings of the spirit. What I do is not for good or evil. Is like electricity in the air, not evil or good, only power. Man makes his evil or good."

"I dreamed of you the night before I saw you in church. When the nigger was killed."

"It is well," Mozelle said.

She came to him and touched his hair and face as she had done long ago. "Do you have a job?"

"I work on the docks unloading packets."

"You will have dinner here tonight," she said. "I will give you money, and tomorrow you will quit your job and come here again."

The next day he came to her house directly from the docks, holding in his overalls his last day's wages and the thirty-dollar bank note Mozelle had given him. He knocked, and the maid appeared at the wicket. "Wait there," she commanded. He paced the deep front gallery nearly an hour before the door opened.

This time he was taken to another bedroom in the house where Mozelle sat in a kimono. Behind her, a copper man with a moustache and centrally parted hair stood, squinting, marcelling her hair. A burly Italian lay in the bed behind them, snoring, wrapped in a sheet. The room was smoky from singed hair and curling wax. "You going to just stand in the doorway?" Mozelle cried out in a colorature soprano. "Come," she said. "This is Jean-Claude."

His eyes smarted.

The man's image bled through the room's haze. His face cracked into a deferential grin. He blew on his curling tongs.

"That is Salvatore on the bed. You'll meet him later," she told him. Then to Jean-Claude: "This is Gabriel. Gabriel will work around here for Mozelle. I'm going to show him how to take care of my yard and keep the rough edges trimmed."

The hairdresser laughed at the double meaning.

"Go down to the kitchen and tell Lorraine I said to show you your room," she said.

Going down the hall he heard Jean-Claude sigh. "That is a fine-looking *blanc*, Mam'selle. You know how to pick them."

His room was a shadowy place at the back of the house. He imagined a succession of young men had lived there. Except for the poster of a naked showgirl that was nailed to a wall, the bed was the most prominent object in the room. His few belongings were packed into a carton on the bed. Mozelle had ordered his things brought from his room on Toulouse Street.

He did become Mozelle's yardman. He reformed the jungled grounds, aerating and thatching the soil. He planted burning bush and large, showy Scotch broom, flush with the street. He watered and cultured the high-walled garden at the north corner, on which, past huge pomegranate, pear and lemon trees, lay a wheel-shaped tract of medicinal herbs. It was here he met Mozelle each evening as the sky reddened and cooled.

She carefully taught him to identify those plants used for healing and divination and told him of their different uses. She showed him how the roots and herbs were grown, gathered and dried.

"The way to learn the herb is by its smell," she said, sitting in the midst of the fragrant wheel. The noise of her earbells trailed off into the gloom. "You must not be afraid to get right against the earth. The plant is good. It is the manifestation of clarity of will." She reached for a leaf of nightshade. "I invoke the help of the herb, the root, when I reach for power. Mozelle has never gone unanswered."

He was harvesting mugwort leaves when he heard a whir and saw a black snake come wriggling up through a pile of twigs.

He closed his shears slowly and took aim to stab the snake.

Mozelle shouted at him, lunging for the shears. "Do not kill him. This is his plant. He has helped the mugwort grow to fulfill power. See how the plant grows leaning to the north? The snake is a magical creature. No one can resist the power of the snake." She picked up the snake and watched it flow down her arm.

Salvatore Chinzano was Mozelle's house bully, backer and common-law husband. He was a husky, little man in his thirties with a baby-smooth face. His trousers were cuffed and creased with braid and satin coming down the outer seam. He wore his ebony hair oiled and combed back. To the girls turning tricks in Mozelle's house, he was rat poison in spats. Whenever one of the prostitutes misbehaved, Mozelle had Chinzano beat them. He was always careful not to leave any bruises on the girls.

He had worked his way to the top of a grueling game, from collecting debts on the docks since he was sixteen years old to running hot street hotels where whores rented rooms by the hour to his partnership with Mozelle in a luxury house.

The girls in the house called him a freak, whispering that Chinzano could only get an erection while eating expensive chocolates from a woman's vagina.

He knew Mozelle had a passion for young studs, and, thinking the preacher boy was another of her tinhorns, he treated him with tolerance mixed with detachment.

"What you think you do when Mozelle get tired of your dick?" Chinzano asked him one morning. It was Friday. They sat in the parlor drinking coffee. Most of the whores were still asleep. Mozelle had gone shopping with Lorraine. He was sorting out the fresh linen. Chinzano counted last night's take with a pistol on the taboret, separating the police and City Hall cuts into envelopes. The house piano man, who had stayed awake sniffing cocaine until dawn, was fingering a Stephen Foster tune.

When the linen was counted and marked, he would deliver the graft to City Hall, then come back and work in the garden. "How do you know I'm fucking her?"

"Sal is no fool. You aint the first kid who cherry Mozelle copped. She never done it to no little preacher before though. You planning on getting back up in a pulpit when she through with you? I guess even preachers got to sow wild oats. Mozelle is a good teacher. Tell me something. You ever eat out a pussy, preacher?" Chinzano roared a concerto laugh, slapping his leg.

"It's too bad, you know, you going to be a preacher, because I tell you—no shit—you got a good future in houses like this one. You would be a hell of a fancy man, little preacher. You just the kind of stud the whores really shake they ass for. You see how Mozelle's girls always tease with you and make up excuses to talk to you? They want you. They want you to fuck the taste out they mouth, I tell you little preacher. I hear them talk about you. And you never going to lose it. I know it. You like me. You going to stay young and keep reminding them of something innocent even when you beat they ass."

Chinzano sat for a long while counting up gold, silver and dollar bills. "Too goddamn bad," he said, shaking his head over the money. "Mozelle tell me about your little church on Flood Street where you preaching to the niggers. If you want to preach, why you want to preach to niggers aint got a pot to piss in? In a few months I move this whole operation up North. We go to New Jersey—Newark. You hear of that place? Little city right before you get to Manhattan. Got everything New York got without all the competition in the rackets. Small sonuvabitch of a town growing fast. Companies moving in every day. Buildings going up all over the place. Even niggers making much money. I visited there last winter and talked around and made contacts. Going to have a house up there for my Mozelle to make this place look like a fifty-cent cribjoint. I swear on the Virgin, New Orleans is dead. Everybody fly. First thing I do I get up there I hire a real colored jazz band. Going to put my nigger band in red jackets and let them wail with that real whorehouse music. The blue bloods and state capital boys we got backing this place don't know shit about real music. *That's* what they want to hear." He shut his eyes a moment and scowled listening to the piano man.

"You know, I have my eyes on you and Mozelle, little preacher. She like you better than the rest of her cherry boys. I know. I figure you last a little longer than the rest of them too. I like to see Mozelle happy. You come with us when we ride the beat up North. You want to preach to niggers, you have a better chance up there. All the dinges with any self-respect left this town anyhow. Even mulattoes like Mozelle, they fly north to pass for white or down Mexico passing for Spanish."

She came up to him unheard, fingering the edges of her shawl. Like a ripe moon, her face appeared in the dark. She spread her six-hundred-dollar dress and sat next to him beneath the tree.

Mozelle felt the ground and picked up a persimmon seed. "The persimmon will tell your future," she said. "Take out your pocket knife."

She cut open the seed. A leaf was between the halved seed.

"The leaf is shaped like a spoon. It is well. It means your future is full. It is misfortune when the leaf is shaped like a knife."

He watched her hand twirling the tiny leaf. "How do you know it's my future and not yours?" he asked.

"I have no future and no past. God sent Moses a man of the mountain. He sent Mozelle a woman in New Orleans."

They sat in the garden, noticing every sound, smell and shadow.

At last Mozelle said, "Sal tell me he ask you to come to Newark with us. You will come?"

"I haven't decided. I thought about it. I want to go . . . where you go." He hesitated. "I need to think on it."

"Too much thinking will make you confuse. Salvatore likes you, in his way. He never like any of my *petits haubans*. He is not fond of any man—the younger the man the more Salvatore despise him. He says I copped your cherry. He calls you my quail, you know. Do you mind?"

He began to feel hot. He felt himself blush.

"They all think you white."

He lowered his head. He loved Mozelle. Yet sometimes he

could not help but be a little ashamed of her. "Why don't you tell them the truth?"

"What truth?" she asked as artlessly as a child. "Let people see what they want. You must know by what you will feel down here, yes." She tapped herself below the rib cage. "Not by so-called truth. This world is illusion, dear one. People here are dreamers, dreaming in the lap of a witch called Time.

"You have not seen much of the world growing up in Sylva's house, going to church with hypocrites. It is all right to read the Bible. It is all right to wish to be a preacher and bring Light. It is well. But men were finding God before there was a Bible to read. But you must read the scripture of your own heart. You must go hand in hand with the spirit and learn this world for yourself. You must go down in the wilderness where nobody pray. Where the fangs of beasts glitter, snapping for your soul. Through living, you will get God. You must come through the gate. The gate is hunger. The gate is lust and sorrow. The gate is fear. You must come through. Then when you speak no one will traverse your authority. They will not sit like dead stones. Your word will pour out fire on them. They will have to move."

He lay in bed turning left and right, unable to fall asleep. He shivered beneath his quilt. In between tending his stiff, curled-up prick he was trying to imagine what life in the North was like. He envisioned an industrial heaven with democratic side-walks brimming with every nationality of Man. A purple sky framed huge, majestic buildings. He knew he would not be able to resist that northern city called Newark, where gas-powered automobiles were plentiful and parks with lakes and fine trees lay in the thick of granite and limestone. Chinzano told him that in the winter men wearing derbies and women in short skirts skated there, gliding on ice-covered swamps and lakes. Newark was irresistible not only because of the strange luxuries he believed he would find there, but because it was where Mozelle was going. He sometimes thought of leaving her to build his church and make his mark, but his love for her had him bound, and so he delayed. Mozelle was his starpoint, his core without which there could be nothing. Her voice had become the sound of destiny. Her terrifying beauty was the foundation of religion. If Chinzano did not take her away to Newark, he feared he might stay with her forever in her ark of a house, watching her whores' linen, mixing drinks for her clients and taking care of her still, stolid garden.

He was turning in the sleepless trance when he heard someone at his door. He watched Mozelle come into his room like a cool ghost in her peignoir. Her breasts were smeared with red powder.

Getting him from his bed, and him not knowing for certain if he was dreaming or stepping from the bed into the phenomenal world, she brought him to her room at the top of the house. The furniture—the bed, tables, cabinets, the screen—and the pretty dresses were gone. In the east corner of the room was an altar blazing with black candles and coconut shell lamps lit with floating flames. In the middle of the altar inside an exquisite silver cage, a snake turned and writhed.

Mozelle fell down on one knee in front of the altar mumbling. She wore a head rag tied with seven knots, the points sticking up straight. She took two bones and held them like a cross. Her body glowed with sweat.

She put the bones in his hands. "These bones come from Old Sylva's tomb. I took them myself," she spoke proudly. "This one come from his chest. This one come out of his left hand, the dreaming hand. Old Sylva flown the world. Bones and dust are all that is left. These bones are Sylva's essence and accumulation—Sylva-will, strength, and mind. He will help you. The living will not serve the dead, but the dead must serve the living."

Mozelle let him hold the bones, then she removed them and

placed a large emerald in his hand. "Here is emerald, the egg, the mystery. It will give the power to understand the particular and open the stream of mind. Let your mind be clear so you can realize your potential. Let your heart and mind be in the same place."

She pulled a snow-white pigeon from a basket. The bird flew in her grasp. Mozelle dipped a machete into the pigeon's throat. She made him drink the pigeon's blood, and she drank after him. She placed the soft bird flesh inside the cage.

Fearfully he watched the snake strike and devour the bird. He felt cold and hot shivers roil from the base of his spine. He ran to the door and vomited in the hallway. When he returned to the room the snake calmly waved its body inside the cage, sheened with blood. Mozelle was before the throne of the snake, the gilt-edged light glittering in her face. He sat at the other side of his mother in front of the small altar. Repulsion cooled within him, then vanished. Stillness, like a sustainable love, bolstered him. He stared at the snake for hours. Mozelle began to sing as the first light flashed on the walls, and the candles and shell lamps began to go out one by one with a heavy smoke. Her song was a sweet wordless cry spilling out the narrow space between morning and night, and he knew she had become— her eyes gleaming white like new moons—the oracle of the snake. He received the song. It was as though a thunderbolt or the sun or some other supreme light had entered him and was spreading its illumination to the world from his heart.

He fell asleep in the room. He awoke when it was dusk-dark. The room was empty except for a snakehide stuffed with spices and jewels lying on the floor with the two human bones. He picked up the bones and lay the snakehide about his shoulders.

Her face flashed like an ornament in the night of time. He saw Mozelle move inside the bedroom-office at the very top of the house at 99 Avon Avenue in Newark. She was surrounded by high quarter-windows that allowed the moon and sun to enter but prevented neighbors from looking in on her. The room was an entire half-story above four flights of stairs. There was a rust-eaten balcony off the room. Many years ago the door to the balcony had been sealed.

It was almost dawn. The house was locked. The whores were asleep. The overnight johns had been tucked in. Mozelle tread the room holding a glass of Scotch whiskey against the hum of ghost-voices and hellish coon dogs howling inside her head. That night for the first time in her life, she told him much later, she felt old. Almost instantly, white strands had appeared in her luscious hair. She began to support charities with her fortune. She founded a neighborhood center in Newark's slum-ridden Third Ward. She sponsored free dinner programs for the poor. She had even begun to make her way each Sunday to a private pew in the back of the Cathedral of the Sacred Heart in Branch Brook Park. Mozelle was seeking good works as though works were salvation, but her soul would not rest contented until she found Daddy Poole and brought him back to Newark.

He had stayed in Newark for three years in the sandstone house she had bought for him on Prince Street. He opened a series of storefront churches: There was the Temple of the Fire Baptized, the Church of the Transfigured Christ, the Sanctified Holy House of God, the Church of the Metaphysical Fire and the Free Church of Ethiopian Jews—all appearing in fast succession in the Third Ward, each failing more profoundly than the last. His sermons did not attract great attendance or large cash offerings. He could not set a church to weeping and rocking the way these diamond-flashing northern preachers could. They knew how to rock their praise houses with singing-screaming sermons, dervish spins and mighty dance steps. They gave prophecies, blessed rags and healings. They knew how to build a feeling until the congregation beat the floors with their heels and retched in every muscle, overturning benches, crying to God.

But he had not learned to work the illusions of a great gospel show. His congregations complained he was only "playing church" and "didn't have nothing but the words." After his last church closed, he sneaked off in the middle of the night. He left all the lights on in 28 Prince Street. He left a pot of coffee brewing and the icebox filled with food.

Mozelle felt death around her in her room. She had never been sick a day of her adult life, but she knew, the way other people perceive the change of the season, that she did not have long to live.

Mozelle was dying, and she was not sick.

God is a time-god, the words rang off inside her head, *and He is killing every one of us by the time.* She looked over the rim of her whiskey glass, where she saw, reposed on the surface of the liquid, her own reflection. Her hair hung loose gathering moonlight.

She sat her drink on the nightstand. She got on her knees and, from a steel trunk she kept locked beneath her bed, produced a homemade map of the world. The richly colored map resembled a game board. She took a diamond hatpin from the top of the chiffonier and fastened the map to the wall.

Mozelle held the hatpin, bringing him into her mind, feeling for him with her hand. She shut her eyes to concentrate on him better. She was a long while standing there, until she heard birds singing in the elms just below her window. At last she sank the pin into the map and dropped her hand. Her eyes opened. She had stuck the pin into Africa. Africa! He could not be in Africa. Mozelle could not concentrate. Could not think.

She folded the map and locked it away again with the old feather fans and boxes of face powder inside the trunk. Replacing the trunk beneath the bed, down on her knees, she reached for the small of her back. She stood and walked stiffly to the steam radiator and opened the valve. She went to the Victrola and cranked up Jelly Roll Morton's "New Orleans Joys."

The next night she stood at her map again holding the jeweled hatpin, now at midnight, the time which tells all. She closed her eyes and stretched her arm. Mozelle stuck the pin in the paper. She looked: Mississippi. The diamond at the end of the hatpin turned reddish. "It is well," she said. She relaxed and felt herself enter the jewel with her mind. Light sparkled on all the floors and walls. She heard the rumbling, fast-timing music. Then she heard a voice inside her, inside the jewel:

He had disappeared.

He had a ministry in Harter, Mississippi, where his congregation turned him out for preaching a double ministry and trying to bring the Devil into the pulpit with Christ. The country negroes built him a church house surrounded on all sides by black holly bushes out on Remembrance Road. They gave him horses and money. They fed him in their kitchens and on their front porches. They stocked his store bins from their crops and his smokehouse from the slaughter of their prime animals. He was not with them for a year before he had eight of their unmarried girls pregnant and had taken three wives away from good husbands. Still he had preached that he was acting within the will of God, and performed miracles for them. He would cite the great men of the Old Testament in the Bible—Solomon, David, Moses, Abraham—men who, despite disobedience and imperfection, were transformed by faith in God. By then, his dominion over the negro rim of Harter had become a fact. It was not until he put the snake before them to worship that they set fire to his house.

When the congregation approached the church house for Tuesday prayer service that evening, they noticed the curtains were all closed and the building was dark. They opened the door at his call. The first thing that struck them as they entered was the long serpentine row of burning black candles on the altar. The light threw a lurid cast over the room. He stood at the far wall, in the pulpit, wearing a white robe and a red kerchief tied around his head. He beat a drum and moaned one of their own hymns. They advanced on him slowly, none of them saying a word, just looking in shocked disbelief. Then one of the children saw it, and all of them saw the huge snake, directly before the altar, writhing in blood.

Then they all waited. They left the church and went to their homes. The next morning the old women said, "How you today, Reverend?" when he passed them on his horse on the way into town. The men talked of the crops that had been laid aside and the winter cordwood that was chopped and hauled.

They waited until dark, when he had locked up the church and was alone in his house on Water Street. The women were attending their weekly clubs and circles. Three firebombs were made with explosives bought downriver and hurled into every story of his house. A group of men watched the windows of the house blaze silver-blue, then black, then bright red.

The fire truck came. The house burned rapidly and crumbled to the ground.

The next morning they returned, after the fire marshal was gone, but no trace of him was found in the wreck. The men had watched in the holly bushes around the property to see if he might come running from the burning house. They had brought guns and knives to kill him and put him back into the flames. They saw him enter the house, but no one saw him come out.

He escaped. Disappeared, and yet one of the men swore he had seen a beast with wings last night fly up from the house into the sky.

The girl whom the stranger had brought with him to Harter walked into the river the day after he disappeared.

He had driven a wagon that was painted fit for a carnival with embroidered curtains and four ornamented gleaming white mares. He brought with him in the wagon, pulling along the high bluffs into the center of Harter, a tense, plain-looking girl, barely in her teens, whom he called his wife. She wore long holy dresses and when spoken to lowered her head. She called him Daddy and Mister and worked like his slave in the high grim house he bought behind Main Street. He had business with the white men in town and looked like a white man himself with his green eyes and pearl-pale skin. The girl he called his wife was elderberry-black. She kept her hair covered in a head rag. The same white men in town who used their horsewhips to lash negroes for standing in the road when their buggies passed sat in the storefront of the Harter Rest and Grill, drinking liquor and playing cards, while the stranger sat in their midst, not drinking or playing cards but talking in long ceaseless runs like a mockingbird and studying the movements of their hands.

He did not walk like a white man, Harter's negroes agreed, and no white man could have so ripe a mouth as his or such a fine Ethiopian head. "He walk like a horse rid' by God," the old black women remarked, watching him in the center of town where they came each morning to sell produce or collect and deliver washing. These women waited for the time when he would come to them with his kisses which they knew were sweet and call them Mother and give them tokens of store-bought candy and gingerbread. They would bring him into their shacks out at the end of Remembrance Road, calling him Son, and serve him pecan pie and the ice cream they made on their camellia-covered porches. In their homes, they would finger the doilies on their haggard chairs and tell him about their dead husbands, their grown children and their Jesus.

When he came to Remembrance Road, where they lived hidden from the eyes of the white people, in his crazy wagon with that child-woman seated beside him stock-still as an Indian, it was not as the old women had expected. It was March and the azaleas were blooming. He had been in Harter for three months.

A crowd gathered to watch him coming down their road in a storm of red-purple dust. He stopped the wagon at a distance from them and just stood there beside a tall holly tree, looking at them watching him. Women held their babies in the still dusk air to see him. The old men and their sons were the first to approach him. The women hung back, catching his deep voice from the air. He had a miracle of a voice. His voice was like hands lying over them, knowing them, comforting them.

He did not want to know about the bream, bass and perch the men were catching in the yellow Mississippi. He was not interested in the crops that were set in the ground, or if there would be deer or fox to hunt that year, or how the men hunted. He said his name was Poole, *Reverend* Sammy C. Poole, and the C didn't stand for anything. He asked, looking over the heads of the men to include the women, "Who among you are sick and need healing?"

He came back in the dead of winter driving a Hudson Phaeton. He had on a Palm Beach suit, a black broad-brimmed hat and silver-tipped shoes.

Mozelle whispered, "Have mercy," when she saw him walk into her house. Then her laughter rose up like a reborn well. She put her arms around him and brought his head to hers. He smelled the nape of her neck. It was the same Mozelle. They looked at each other a long moment. He was the one who had changed. He believed it was so, but now seeing how Mozelle looked at him with reverence, he knew he was, at last as if by some final and absolute evolution, perfected.

"You look good, baby."

"I'm doing all right. It's nothing but the salvation of God."

She turned inside the bay of lead-glass windows in the parlor and looked at the Phaeton parked outside. "This is my salvation," she said, turning and moving to touch him. "You have come back to start another church, no? It is well. You are worthy."

"The work's been done in my life, Mozelle. I even changed my name while I was away this time. I'm Sam Poole now."

"There is more power in names than people imagine." Her gaze remained on him, reading him. "So, tell me. I want to know everything. Two years is long. No word."

"There'll be time. I just . . . traveled. The last place I went was Madagascar."

"Where is this place?"

"At the end of the world off the tip of southern Africa."

She colored and smiled. "The old gods come from Africa. I was feeling for you on my map."

"We move together."

Her smile looked as fragile as life. "I took sick this last fall. Thought I might die. Doctors still don't know what I had. I'm leaving Newark."

"You can't leave. I need you here."

"I know you do, and I'll help you, but I've got to leave Newark."

"Where are you going?"

"You will know."

He followed her to the back of the house and down a flight of stairs behind a false wall. The strains of a piano playing met them on the stairs.

Mozelle opened a door on a wide, glimmery room. A crystal ball suspended from the ceiling threw particles of light on gamblers sitting at tables playing roulette. A black piano man conjured a slow rocking jazz march on a mirrored piano. To the side, prostitutes danced with johns and sat on sofas. There was a long bar with a dark marble counter and shining bottles.

"It's a whole new thing since you were last in town." In that light her face turned golden. She brought him to a table in the back. A waiter dressed in a mandarin jacket brought glasses and a bottle of champagne, then disappeared. The music changed to a free, easy boogie. "Wait till the piano player snaps off 'Wolverine Blues.' I have a girl who comes on later who sings like a natural bird. Wears nothing but a feather, and she's a stepper. She has the moves to put Florence Mills, Jo Baker, all those classy jazzbos and crooners, cold out of business."

She gave him an out-of-this-world look. "Tell me something. Did you go back to New Orleans?"

"I spent a day there. Elodie has passed. Old Sylva's house is now city property. It's just as well. I don't want it. I walked through Congo Square. They call it Beauregard Square now. The Mardi Gras hadn't long been over. The streets were a mess."

"Iberville Street, Basin Street, Rampart Street," she chanted. "Dumaine Street, where the negroes used to dance to the beat of hambones beating pork barrels. Lord, I tell you, sometimes I miss my city. I walk down her streets in my dreams and hear those spasm bands at Congo Square playing the first music I ever learned to love. Making that bamboula music with drums covered with cowhide, playing a jackass's jawbone through their teeth. The stiff-back nigger Creole gals dancing the juba shouting *Dansez! Fous-moi le camp!*' Street hollers ringing through the streets. Lord, I've thought of going back to look at her, but I know I would only cry if I saw New Orleans now. No pleasure in looking for the past, is it? Got to move forward. I found my place in this city, and now I own it."

Mozelle leaned back sipping gold champagne. "That's why I'm glad you come back. Newark is opening up and I want you to try again, bigger than before. And you will have success this time. Not only Newark but more. I'm going to France. Montmartre. The *haut monde noir* and many artists, writers and show people have a colony there. I hear it is made like the Quarter fifty years ago. *That* is a place where a gal could live out her last days with tone and style. I want you to take over here."

"This?" He turned to take in the room.

"I know this is not your style. But Chinzano will stay on here. No trouble between him and me. I'm just getting too old to have a husband. Mozelle need a *man* now. I finally found the cherry boy I been looking for. Sixteen-year-old gold-skin who fuck like a dream. I'm taking him with me.

"Chinzano wants to stay. He's part of a syndicate here that ran in three million dollars' worth of liquor last year. Now the city builds an airport out in the meadowlands. It takes forty ships and six months for Chinzano's men to get their liquor into Port Newark. It come down through Canada from a French island. If they get into that airport, they will triple their money by bringing the liquor in on planes."

"Long as Prohibition holds out."

"That's right, and it's too good a business to die soon."

"I don't see where I fit in."

"But you are the key to the kingdom. You can face for Chinzano's whole operation. Sal is a man with a program. Always was. He always like you too in spite of himself. He want to set you up this time with your own church. Not some common storefront but a cathedral like the colored never see before. Grander than the praise temples of Father Divine and Reverend Becton."

"Working for Salvatore Chinzano?"

"Working for yourself. You run your game any way you want to. Plus you take over this house—because it is mine and I want you to have it. You do anything you want with it. If you want you can fire the whole star line and shut the place down. You take Sal in as your partner on your church business. He gets fifty percent for the first five years, and a smaller percent after that. Religion is a fortune in these northern cities."

His head was lowered with thoughts. In no time hardly his face lifted, fixed with his decision. "Where is Chinzano now?"

"That's him over there."

He looked across the lively room at two men seated beside a

fire door. Chinzano sat meditatively peeling an orange on a silver tray. His waistcoat was open, showing off a diamond-patterned shirt and a dotted tie.

"Who's that with him?"

The other man wore a hat and coat and had a cigar planted in the center of his mouth.

"A city commissioner. He's been on the house payroll since we got here. Sal has him working on the mayor to let the syndicate, invest in the airport."

When construction of Newark Airport was completed, Salvatore Chinzano sat in the dignitary's box at the dedication ceremony along with the city commissioners, a local watch manufacturer and a senator. A crowd had gathered to hear the mayor call the sixteen thousand feet of runway Newark's "link to the twentieth century."

At 99 Avon Avenue racketeers from Newark, New York and Philadelphia were throwing a party for Sam Poole with a giant red cake and an all-star jazz band. Daddy got out in the middle of the dance floor and did the Charleston with a line of twelve of his whores. The clarinets went crazy. He fell back on a high-stepped stool pouring champagne in his hair and kissing his sporting girls. "Ah, Lord," he wailed, "I'm going to give you gals a hell of a home."

7.

≈≈ "You a conk-buster, baby. I'm getting sick of fooling with you. Your father just Georgiaed you same as he did everybody else. Only everybody else learned. You just won't learn. Daddy is a disgrace, laying back in Twenty-eight steeped in his own shit and piss, talking to hisself all out of his mind. That man don't know if he living or dead. Don't know if he a man or a baby. He don't know if he in 1981 or 1901. And you more mixed up than he is. I'm sick of you and your stupid shit. I hope your social worker find out you working and cut off your checks. It might make you wake up, Martha. You too dumb to draw a breath much less a damn check."

Peanut put on her bra and fastened the snaps. "It's getting too hard to make it in this world to be walking around trying to live some bullshit fairy tale. Times too hard. The times is a killer, Martha. All you got to do is go in that kitchen and look at the headlines on the newspapers to see where the world is going. That shit you talk aint going to do nothing for you, and it aint

148

going to put food in your baby's mouth neither. The biggest downfall of negroes is they always waiting for God to bust the sky, but I aint got no use for the idea of God. You got to make your own help in this world. Aint no mercy or magic. I know, because I lived. You pay for everything you get, and if you don't get nothing you still have to pay. Life come down to money. That is all Sam Poole was about—grinding up that glory roll. That's all that separate a man from animals anyway. You used to have sense. I don't know what happened to you."

She went in the bathroom and left the door open. She stood at the medicine-cabinet mirror arranging bobby pins in her wig. "And you can say whatever you want about me, but Daddy aint never had *me* brainwashed." She stared at herself in the mirror as if looking for something lost. "I was the best street whore your father ever had. I was younger than you now when he turned me out to sex. He had his whores living in six different houses in Newark, and I was over all the girls in my house. We was young. We was in love with your father. You going to think I'm a lie, but he used to fuck every one of us at least one or two times a month. That was before Sarah Anderson come on the scene. *Once or twice a month.* I'm talking at least thirty girls. And you couldn't pull no dyke moves in his stables. Daddy didn't allow no women loving each other. You had to love him, honey, and you don't know what that love was all about. You had to take an ass-kicking from him and still jump up and say, 'I love you, Daddy.' You had to get out there and trick for him if you was half-dead to prove your love, and if you couldn't make enough money tricking, you would pick pockets or gamble for it, hustle it any way you could. I was pulling down a thousand dollars' worth of tricks a day. Don't think I ever saw none of that money neither. But I was gassed. I was in a groove. I had me a car, boss clothes and twenty-five wigs. Every now and then I used to drive up to New York and go to the shows and clubs, you know, where nobody didn't know what the hell I was.

"Daddy set me up in my own apartment over in the South Ward. He let me decorate it the way I wanted with a record player and colored lights. I had a blue mink coat and a blue diamond ring. Then, when Sarah Anderson come on the scene, he started treating all his whores like we was second-class citizens. I hate Sarah Anderson, and I hate her mother too. Them two, old mother and daughter, used to be thick as thieves till about the time Daddy broke up his church. Both of them got real close ways. They used to be sitting up on Sister Sarah's porch all the time in the summer like two queens talking they soft tight-lipped talk. I never could stand Sarah, putting on all her highborn airs when she aint nothing but what I am and not even as good at it. And as far as her dried up pussy mother, that Savannah, is concerned, my mother gave me all the reason I would ever need to go out there and shoot that old woman dead in the street."

Martha got up and moved away from the chair. She stopped at the window. She determined to let Peanut talk herself out of words. Peanut was a living history book when it came to Newark, Daddy, Sister Sarah and Sister Savannah. She told the same stories over and over. Peanut did not care how many times she repeated herself when it came to the past and how things had happened in Newark. She knew how to play past the words and make a larger and larger picture.

"I grew up on the story, and my mother told it to me so careful you would have thought every word of it could save my life—just like I hoped the things I tell you might save you. Maybe it did save me. I don't know. It sure aint stop me from wanting to be your father's whore when I was a kitty. For a hip kitty coming up in Newark that was the highest ground you could reach for. One thing is sure though, it saved me from ever being Daddy's fool.

"The yellow girl—that's what she was called, Sister Savannah, and in 1928 she was your father's main queen. She would be stretched out in the bed reading the papers in Twenty-eight Prince Street talking on the phone to New York, Chicago or Philadelphia.

"It was late, the cook was making supper on the gas stove in the second-floor kitchen, and the yellow girl, that 1928 early dark night, still aint have on nothing but a camisole. Sometime she would lay in Daddy's bed, morning, noon and the best of the evening, drinking ice coffee, talking on the phone in one voice, yelling for her bedpan in another and telling her upstairs girl to tell the downstairs girl to put more coals in the furnace. She liked a hot, burning house.

"She took all them papers, like the *Newark Herald, News,* the New York papers, *The Messenger, Opportunity* and *Crisis.* It wasn't your father reading them papers. It was the yellow girl.

"I used to sit in our front room with Mama long before I was old enough to start school, me in a red-covered child's chair and her sitting in a split-bottom cane chair she brung with her from the South. The same chair I saw her sitting in every day I knew her. She would be talking in her pea-dove voice, taking her time, and I was just sitting there listening, looking at her—all twisted and bent up in her chair—her dead eyes looking off clean back to 1928, using her words to make a spotlight for me to see the faces of her enemies so they'd be my enemies too. So when I was big enough to leave that room and go out into them same long, burning streets she had stepped out into when she was young and fine, I would know and guard my soul from them what would devour it."

Martha stood by the window studying her hands. She only pretended to listen. If she could not stop Peanut from telling, over and over, all she knew about Daddy, at least she could will herself to stone.

"The yellow girl would be talking to stockbrokers in New York over the phone or Bamberger's or John Wanamaker's department store in Philadelphia, ordering up expensive things most negroes aint have and never seen. It was all the time some kind of business on the phone, never talking to no friends. She aint have no friends.

"My mother had come on at seven o'clock that morning, and by now she had sweated out the edges of her hair. Even the ribbons in her hair had gone so limp she finally took them out and twisted her hair back off her face. They was running her ragged from the back of the house to the front, then up and down them cellar steps. The doorbell went off every other minute. The yellow girl wasn't seeing nobody today. So Mama was telling them 'Sister Sparks is engaged.' *Sister* if the callers was black. *Miss* if they was white. Then there was deliveries at the back door. Your daddy must have owned a diamond mine. The packages wasn't just coming from Bamberger's, Wanamaker's and the New York stores. There was packages from all over the world. She looked in some of the boxes. There was gold-threaded and beaded material for dresses, carved boxes and jewelry, wigs, caviar, crates of champagne and big, fifty-dollar boxes of chocolate. Fresh flowers came into Twenty-eight Prince Street three times a day. Men in overalls marched through that kitchen holding crystal tanks filled with shiny colored fish and set them up with lights in the parlor. And the food what come into that house was enough to feed the neighborhood: smoked meat, mangoes, bananas on stalks, sacks full of grains and spices. Carpenters was in and out the back door, cussing and talking loud and pinching for her behind. The vestibule, halls and all the first-floor closets was being papered. Mama was supposed to clean up whenever the working crews had a break. 'You aint so beautiful you can't work.' That was what the upstairs girl kept hollering at Mama. And Mama—Miss Mattie Albertina Earle—was fine. I know. I seen a picture of her she had took when she first came up North at a Chinese photo place. She was about six feet tall before her neck got twisted. Bold eyes. Smooth, gold hands she still had even when I knew her, after Savannah was through with her.

"She had to be at least as beautiful as that yellow Savannah laying upstairs on her ass all day talking on the telephone. They was about the same age. And Newark was full of all kinds of fine black women looking for a home. They was four girls in service at Twenty-eight Prince Street—all of them ex-whorehouse girls with stacked bodies and pretty faces. So Mama couldn't help from wondering what your father—and you know he was pretty then—was doing, going to bed every night with a one-leg. Him and Savannah wasn't married. And he a preacher living with a woman with a different last name. Down South people would make a preacher live according to rules, but up North negroes was breaking rules, and they was glad to have a new-time preacher.

"Mama was down in the basement shoveling coal into the furnace. She was down there hauling the ash bucket, steady cussing Savannah under her breath. 'It don't make no damn sense,' telling herself, 'lazy yellow bitch.' She couldn't stop thinking about the yellow girl, the peg leg. Sister Savannah come from a town somewhere in Georgia, Mama heard some-where, but not Savannah, Georgia. Might be Clayton or Wrens, Georgia. Sister Savannah talk like a white lady, but negroes in Newark said she had the deep, down home, heathen ways—said she buried things and conjured against people. Talk had it her missing leg was buried in a baby coffin in the white-people cemetery out in Orange.

"'Crazy, yellow bitch,' Mama say, spitting and shutting the furnace door. 'Sam Poole coulda done better than your ass. Preacher and a one-leg. It aint nothing but freakish. 'Shit,' she say, 'if I could get him to just ride *me* for one night . . .'

"There wasn't no reason to think that night wasn't coming too. In 1928, before what happened, Mattie was a woman what knew how to use her face and her body against a man. She'd only been working in your father's house a few days and Sam Poole was already gunning his eyes on her every time he was coming in from his office on Broome Street and she was going off work. The old sad-breath Jew what owned the employment agency where Savannah hired her had set Mama up in a seven-room apartment on Waverly Avenue. Mama was seeing her lovesick Jew every Tuesday night and a Polish dock worker was coming to see her on Thursdays. Plus she had her a sweet beginner brown for Saturdays and Sundays. Couldn't none of her men come to see her neither unless they brung her something. Mattie was a wheeler from the word go, and I'm just like her.

"'Who you speaking with down there?!' Mattie looked up. It was the yellow girl at the top of the cellar stairs, been standing up there all the while listening to Mama cuss her. Savannah had on a red feather headdress. The upstairs girl was standing behind Savannah eating grapes and a roasted turkey wing.

"'Who you speaking with down there?'

"Mama say, 'No one,' so scared she aint squeeze in time and peed on herself. She felt her own piss sting the inside of her thighs and run by her knees. 'I wasn't saying nothing, Sister Sparks,' she say. 'How you this evening?'

"'Come to me,' Savannah say, raising her walking stick a little off the floor. She step back and let Mama reach the top of the stairs. Savannah Sparks tap Mama with the stick. Mama fall down fourteen steps and snap her neck."

Rage rose and fell in Peanut's voice. "That was Savannah's doing—not your father's—but Savannah's. They was a pair—her and Daddy. She probably the only woman he ever had was strictly his match. They say when he got sick with that first stroke along before his church come apart, it was Savannah who put it on him. Her and Daddy lived together three years into the Depression, but Savannah, she never once set foot in one of

Daddy's churches for nothing. Aint nobody in this town ever known her to worship nothing but a dollar with all them ragged pieces of houses she still renting out on this hill and that restaurant she still run over there on Boston Street. Aint nobody never fucked with that cold-blooded bitch moving on her wood leg. Not even your father.

"Mama said first they thought she was dead with that broke neck, but it was Savannah who nursed her right there in Twenty-eight Prince Street without doctor or preacher. And who that yellow bitch think she was but something awful and mighty enough to kill my mama just for cussing her and then bring her back to life so she could live out the rest of her days bent over like she looking for something up in a corner of the ceiling with her hair turned pure white right after her fall so that Mattie always look like an old woman by the face and by her puffed out snowy hair but never—not even by the time she slept on out of this world—by her hands.

"And when she was turned into some kind of half-alive statue of Savannah's meanness, Savannah decided she wanted to keep Mama. So Mama lived in the third floor of Twenty-eight Prince Street until 1932 like something strange you would bring back from a trip to a wild uncivilized country. And that's just what my mama was to Savannah, only that wild country was inside Savannah's heart. Mama was just a well-cared-for thing now that her bold life and sexy sassiness was damaged. Mama called them good times, from the start of the Depression till Roosevelt came in, when she was living up inside your father's house. I guess that's what first taught me people was made for joy and will find it anywhere just like the niggers still laughing and making babies on this gutted-out hill, and there is probably people loving it in Hell, burning and *loving it* in they racked soul.

"Of course, the Depression aint put a damper on Daddy's hot party. Daddy made his first million dollars in 1930. And the more money Daddy was making, the more ways Savannah was finding to spend it. She bought Mama all kinds of South American birds and a Victrola so she could hear a stack of Caruso records. That's who Savannah loved—Caruso—and that white man's tenor voice used to all the time be booming through Mama's room. Savannah would come up there with Mama and they would smoke opium—used to call it kicking the gong— and listen to that Dago sing, and sometime, Mama said, Savannah used to play with her pussy.

"Savannah split from your father around 1932 and moved out into her house on Hillside Place. Savannah and Daddy aint had much to do with each other after that far as nobody could tell and people seem to forget—or the old ones what remember just died away—that there was a time Savannah and Daddy Poole slept in the same bed. I don't think even Sarah know her mama used to be Daddy's Sheba before she had her turn."

Peanut put baby powder down the front of her bra. "Savannah arranged to have Mattie moved out of Twenty-eight before she left. Mama aint have no people in Newark so Savannah bought her a house by Krueger Brewery where I grew up. Savannah fixed a bank account after the war for Mama to draw on for the rest of her life. When Mama died my brother Ollie—a prettier negro you wouldn't want to see and *crazy* about white women—tried to get at some of that money but it all went back to Savannah Sparks.

"Once Mama was moved from Twenty-eight, she aint see Sister Savannah no more. Sarah must have been born somewhere around before her mother was living with Daddy or, for all I know, Daddy could be her father, but Savannah had her sent down South to be raised with some of her Georgia people right after she was born. But now Savannah had Sarah brung back to Newark and was rearing the girl herself on Hillside Place.

"Crippled up like she was, Mama still had her men friends here and there. They would come to her. Two of her men slipped up, though, and Mama had two children. Aint neither one of us of Mama's children know who our daddies was but some bip-bam-thank-you-ma'am poppas who would unzip they big trousers in front of a paralyzed woman in a dank front room but wouldn't stay around after they got they freakish nut long enough for nobody to find out they was doing it to a deformed woman.

"But she was somebody you had to respect. There was something about her what went all inside you and stayed there like one of them songs from down home. Mattie was from hunger and hurt, and she could draw you right into her heart whether you was a no-account lover or the insurance man what came on Mondays or one of the church people used to visit her and pray for her. Them eyes of hers, you knew, had seen the homeland of the soul, seen it by a rough treacherous way. You couldn't help but respect her, setting up in that room on Waverly by all her plaster statues of Jesus, the Virgin, and Saint Jude. I aint never going to forget her. She was whore, mama, woman and monster—all them things in one. Mattie Earle was a *terrible* woman, and she was a champion."

Martha leaned inside the window. She coolly studied the lines inside the palms of her hands. *Stone,* she told herself.

"When Mama seen how I grew up to love running the street, she'd tell me, 'Daughter, there aint nothing in them streets.' And she knew what she was talking about too. When I think about how she come to Newark from Jacksonville, Florida, traveling alone when she was twenty years old, dreaming she was going to end up with a husband to give her everything, and she wasn't going to have to do nothing but lay around in silk tap panties and eat Dutch candy. Working, in the beginning, scrubbing floors for fifteen cents an hour. Finally getting into Sam Poole's house where she felt like God was fixing to crown her with glory. Then turned up like a woman for the freak show with that crooked neck and twisted spine. I was her baby child, and the doctors couldn't believe how easy she delivered. Mattie name me Willa Mac Earle, but she never call me that. She call me Peanut; she said because I was born in the world so tiny and looking so full of possibilities.

"But I wasn't a damn bit of good. I went on straight to your father soon as I got out in the bar life. All you could hear if you was a girl growing up in the life in Newark back then was Daddy Poole, his Cadillacs and his women. When I come out into the street world it was a day of men—not like it is today. All them process-haired, sharp-dressing daddies was running whores and running games, but most of them wasn't nothing but a dick too big for they pants. Seemed to me back then Daddy Poole was more than a thousand men.

"Sure, he was handsome, and nobody had the clothes your father used to wear, but to me the most sexy thing about him was his voice. You could hear him preaching over the radio on Sunday nights. And he used to be at Mr. Wonderful's when it was an all-night rhythm and blues bar. That was where the real rough hellbound soldiers too full of evil to even enter a church might get to see Daddy. He'd be sitting back in the back room like a king. You couldn't hardly see him for all the women what was around him. It was always smoky there, and sometimes I'd be looking in there all night and maybe not see no more of him than a diamond-flashing finger or his mustard-colored hand smoothing down the back of his hair. I was wearing so much makeup I musta looked like a freak. I knew I aint had what a lot of them other women had—nice breasts and a big behind—but I was determined to be one of your father's women just the same. I was just a skinny kid with—in them days—long hair and a cute face. I had big eyes. There was a singer was singing at Mr. Wonderful's named Leavima Hall—hollerer, I should say instead of singer, but she had what it took to please the crowd what came to that place, and you had to be loud to get over all the noise always going on in there—sometimes fighting and cutting. Daddy was sweet on Leavima. She was his main queen at the time. So I went to work on her. I'd hang out in there till closing time, then I'd go up to the stand and tell her how much I liked her singing and shaking. I guess she thought I was all right, because sometime when Daddy wasn't going to spend the night with her, Leavima would let me ride over to her apartment in the Cadillac with red bomber taillights Daddy gave her. She'd cook pepper steaks for us with mustard greens. I might press her clothes and straighten up her closets—I loved to look at all her nice things—or I might wash out her stockings. Leavima always kept plenty of reefer, and she showed me how to smoke it, but I aint like it because it just made me silly. She sang the rocking stuff for the people at Mr. Wonderful, but Leavima could sing the hell out of just about everything. She used to sing real nice blues to me over at her apartment sometime, real light and sassy stuff. She'd be rocking back and forth like she was doing it with a fine, easy lover, her eyes would be closed: 'My daddy rocks me, rocks me with a steady roll, every time he rock me, he sa-tis-fies my soul.' She could make them blues sound almost like spirituals.

"After a while Leavima started to pay me to be her personal maid. It wasn't long before I got to be there in the apartment when Daddy come around. He aint liked Leavima smoking as much reefer as she did, and that's what they would fight about. All the drugs he helped bring in Newark and couldn't stand for her to smoke a damn reefer. She'd try to hide it, but you could smell it no matter what she do, the smell be all in her clothes and hair. Regardless how much Daddy would be on her for getting high, Leavima would stay tore up just the same. I believe her getting high was just her way of dealing with not having no real life. She sang and did her hip-working moves at the night-club seven days a week. She'd come back to her crib and wait for your father. She aint never go nowhere much. Daddy aint allow her to have no friends. She had me put on the payroll, but the biggest thing I was doing was keeping that girl company.

While she was on the set at Mr. Wonderful, she always look like she was having a gas, singing and rattling her long earrings, but that shit aint mean nothing because couldn't nobody touch her up there on that stage. At home she stayed nervous most the time, and by me being around a lot I got to see how much she drank.

"I aint mind drinking with her. We liked Johnny Walker Red. Leavima was good-looking but I knew she was pimp-crazy. You can tell when a woman been hurt by a whole lot of no-good pimps. She *seemed* together, but you could tell there was something inside her was ripping hell out of her. We aint talk that much. It probably wasn't no big thing—no more than what's the matter with a lot of women—feeling like whatever they is and what life give them aint never going to be enough, like they missed the train. And can't never catch up. But when she was on the set she was laid and happening, till one night she had a seizure in the middle of singing a Ruth Brown song. When Daddy brung her back from the hospital he got it out of her she'd been taking over a gram of cocaine a day, and the cocaine had caused her seizure. She'd been blowing that much coke out the fat allowance Daddy give her and trying to clean up her shit by telling him she taking the blow because her nerves is bad. 'Bitch,' Daddy told her, 'your ass is going to be bad if you don't straighten up.' He actually loved that girl. He'd been going with Leavima for damn near a year and he still hadn't turned her out to the pussy game, prostitution. But she just wasn't all there mentally. You had to really be around her to see it. Daddy warned her how he was going to do her if she aint straighten herself up. She aint listen. He couldn't take her shit from her no faster than she would get some more stashed someplace. They say you graduate from one drug to another and in Leavima case it was a true saying. When Daddy caught her skin-popping the Big Boy, that smack, he finally give up on her and cut her loose. He aint have no more use for her then. He closed her out at Mr.

Wonderful's and brung in a jazzy combo. He had Leavima took down to a building by the docks—down in the Neck. All her clothes was took away from her—her car, her jewelry, everything. She was locked in a bathroom down there, and men paid to go in the bathroom and have her. How long Daddy had her doing bathroom tricks or what happen to her after that I don't know and didn't care because when he got rid of her, it was me he put in her place. That was the beginning of me being a whore for Daddy Poole.

"I aint feel no regret for Leavima. That's one thing I always notice how it seems like women can't afford to have no feelings for each other—not only whores and women in the life, but square bitches too. But a man will always side with another man—or a pimp with another pimp—against a woman. A man is always for a man.

"All I knew was I was having a ball. I felt like I was rich or a movie star. I was wearing them fancy form-fitting gowns with the padded bra and padded ass. I had a lavender fox boa, diamond-seamed stockings, long gloves and bare-back pumps. Had the keys to Leavima's Cadillac Coupe de Ville even though I couldn't drive a lick. You couldn't tell me I wasn't into something. I was getting drunk on my damn self. I was high on Peanut. I was a knockout, baby. Tall, fine and skinny. I knew how to *move* in clothes.

"Daddy was keeping me in Leavima's old apartment. He used to come there and fuck me every Monday afternoon. Most of the other time I was just laying around waiting on him. Sometime we would go to Mr. Wonderful or someplace like that, but he always had somebody drive me home before it got good. I don't know what your father knew about love in the supernatural, but he knew about it in the natural. He pop my thing down there so good one time I thought I was coming for a week. He could fuck for a solid hour. By the time he finish working me in them sheets, my hair would be hard as a damn brick, I would sweat just that much.

"We'd go out and I wouldn't never say nothing unless I was spoken to, and when we was going in and out of places, I'd make sure to stay two and three steps behind him. I wouldn't open my mouth to say nothing to nobody, especially if it was something against Daddy. In the apartment it was the same thing. He aint said that much to me if some of his boys was there playing cards with him and drinking unless it was 'bring us some more Coca-Colas' or 'empty these goddamn ashtrays.'

"I was like a slave girl, but I came up fast. The first time he give me a beating he cracked one of my ribs and I still jumped on him and tried to bite his heart out of his chest. It was me and him. He go reaching in his pants for his knife. And I went right for my shiv too. I told him I would cut his ass just as quick as he would cut mine. He aint have no reason for kicking my ass. Just like a man going to try to drive all over a woman just to see how much she will take. After that he said he was putting me in one of his houses and turn me out to the pussy game, because otherwise he knew one of us would kill the other—just depend on who got to it first. I tricked for Sam Poole five years and one morning I just woke up and aint feel nothing no more for him. I aint quit the life—like I said—till I met Jake Means, but right then was where I decided I couldn't have no man over me using me for a wagon. I had to have respect. And it wasn't easy walking out on your father's game neither. Windows to four damn apartments where I was living was shot out before he finally let me alone.

"You can say whatever you want about me, but I *know* where it's at. Archie may fight me sometime, but he know not to go too far with me, or I'll kill him. I wasn't going with Archie but three days when I took my high-heel shoe and knocked him in his foolish fat head for slapping me in public. Another time I throwed hot lye at him for trying to fuck with me. I missed his head by this much. Another thing you see, Archie don't live here. This is Peanut's trip. This is my crib. And I got me a door I can shut in anybody face I choose. Don't nobody got the key to that door but me and the landlord. I can go for myself. I love me some Peanut, baby. The waters of my life been too wide. I love my damn self. I can't have no man mistreating me. Archie bring me his paycheck every two weeks. That's regular money. Plus I'm pulling down two hundred dollars a week in just tips at the Playbar. Plus I'm still collecting disability payments because of my heart condition. I'm a survivor, baby. I keep my act together twenty-four hours every day."

Martha said, "Yeah, it's together, living in a three-room crib without a goddamn refrigerator. You can't even cook in here for all the roaches."

"To hell with you, Martha. It's more than you got. I got a closet full of clothes. What you got to wear outside your maid uniforms? I can outrag and outwig them TV babes. Shit. Come Christmas I'm going to be riding a chocolate-colored Lincoln Continental. You see if I don't. Everything I do going to be funky. And when I get ready I'm going to move off this hill and get me a bad-ass apartment downtown. To hell with you, hear?"

Peanut came out of the bathroom and stood over Martha in the window. It was getting dark. "Shit, what you know anyway? What you ever done but go out and have a baby. Any cow can lay down and get up with a fucking baby. You just lucky your baby wasn't born brain damage from the heroin Silk was shooting hisself with when he knock you up. Man still could be brain damage since a lot of that shit don't show up till much later."

"You don't even know what you talking about. Silk wasn't taking heroin when I got pregnant with Man."

"That's what you say. Go ahead and swear right now that you know for a fact your baby aint brain damage behind having a junkie for a father."

Martha said nothing.

"Yeah, Miss," brayed Peanut, "you so big and loud, I bet you'll shut up now. You just about the biggest goddamn idiot in the world. If you had sense you'd leave Daddy and do something for yourself. It aint too late to make something out of yourself, Martha."

"Something like what? You the goddamn idiot. If Man grow up to be decent I'll be satisfied."

"I wish I could make you see the light, but you won't. If you leave that house you think anybody else be stupid enough to go near your shit-ass father, trying to help him live after all he done to women? Hell, no. Wouldn't nobody be fool enough to care nothing about Daddy now but you."

Martha shook her head slowly. "You wrong, Sister," she said. "You wrong."

Sister Anderson got up from her chair, walking carefully, as if only intending to test the floorboards. She had a flyswatter in her hand. Iphigenia could see her through the corner of her eye, slinking toward the window like a cat.

"Got you!" Sister Sarah cried, slamming the swatter against the screen, and missed.

Patti looked up and saw a green and yellow fly pull itself through the air away from the screen. Sarah angrily withdrew the swatter.

"*Dirty* flies! I told you girls to be careful when you come into my house. Now there's a fly in here. You're always holding the door wide open. Can't you enter a house like people? I've told you, you can't hold the doors open in the summer or flies will get in. Your father is always holding the doors open. Then the house is filled with flies!" Sarah's hands shook until the flyswatter fell to the floor. She gripped too late. She did not pick it up. Patti was going to pick it up, but Iphigenia stopped her. Sister Anderson touched her temples and stroked her forehead.

She ran her fingernails down the screen. "What I really don't understand is why," she said, "those children can't play in front of their own houses. I'm sure they live *somewhere*. Why do they have to play in front of *my* door? Why, in the name of God, does it have to be *my* door?"

Her daughters handled their tea things with new attention. They tried to make their faces steel. They turned their faces into prison houses so no one could see what was locked up inside.

On his huge bed, Daddy snapped his eyes. He saw Mozelle standing by the darkening window. She had on earrings the size of twenty-dollar "Eagles." She stared glassily back at him. At last, she grinned. "Don't worry, baby. You not dying. The Devil's not ready for you yet."

"What the hell you mean I'm wrong?! Your father is going to die. You might as well give it up. You the one who wrong, Martha. He dying. I been feeling it coming. I been waiting for it all my life. That red bastard is going to die. And if you think all the money he had in that house was four satchel bags full of fake gold you a bigger fool than I think you is. He liable to filled them bags with fake gold hisself and put them behind the walls to throw somebody off from finding his real shit. I'd like to take dynamite to Twenty-eight Prince Street. I bet I could find it. It's in there. It's got to be in there. All that money aint gone. Not by a longshot. Daddy musta had a million dollars in just nickels and dimes when he closed his churches. Daddy, Savannah Sparks and Sister Sarah—and now look like it was one more, the marabou, Mozelle—them four was in on a bankroll what piled up for over thirty years. You going to try and tell me it's all gone? If you could just get at it. . . . Shit, you deserve it. All you been through with that man. You better try and get at it."

"You still on that. Aint you tired? I told you he aint got no money. Don't you think I'd know if he did? For Godsake, Sister, let it alone."

"He probably got it hid anywhere."

"He aint hid it."

"Well, what happened to it? It just disappear?"

"Far as I'm concerned it did."

"Somebody got it. I bet Sister Sparks got hers."

"That old lady. Then what she doing still living on Hillside Place?"

"And I bet Sarah Anderson got a heap of it too."

"She aint got no more money than her husband give her."

"Well go ahead then, you so damn smart and can't listen to nobody trying to help you. Just keep on living on the relief and helping that motherfucker fight death."

"He *aint* fighting!" Martha screamed, stepping away from the window. She had wanted to avoid arguing anymore. "He glad to die. Last time I had him in the hospital, he just laugh when the doctors give him three months—five at the most—to live. He say he walking and got up from the hospital bed and put on his coat over his johnny. He said he was walking straight into the kingdom of Heaven even if he got to pay his admission with his life."

"I don't want to hear it, Martha. How the hell he think he going to drag hisself into Heaven with one foot in Christianity and the other in sin? Your father aint never cared about nothing but money and keeping his pecker stuck in some sister's gash. *Nobody* don't know what all he done to get all that power and money, a half-black man in 1904. Or what he had. God is whipping your father. Whipping him down to his soul. Whipping him with sore stripes, baby. What he got? What he aint got by now? Syphilis, TB, cancer, heart disease, cirrhosis of the liver."

"Yeah, well, he aint going to die. Not even much as he ready to die Daddy going to keep living. I know what I'm talking about. You mark my words."

"Martha, you talking like a fool."

"A fool or a player with an ace in the hole. Two damn aces."

"Well, don't go tipping your hand yet, baby, because my money say he going out this same night."

Peanut was collecting the beer cans around the room and putting them in a paper sack.

"People knew your father by a lot of different things. Daddy Poole played a lot of different parts in and out of his time. I bet you don't know your father was ward boss for the Hill during the Depression. If he had been a real white man, I believe the friends he had in City Hall would have made him mayor. I believe that. He controlled most of the jobs in the Third Ward during the thirties, and he agreed with a commissioner they had then that the city ought to send poor blacks back down South. Daddy was tough as any of Newark's white bosses. When he had his quota filled, he'd tell the broke-down women and men, 'Sorry, but I aint hiring no more niggers today.' 'Niggers the worst thing on earth,' that's what he used to say. 'You give one a job, he work a few days, then you don't see him no more. All a nigger wants out of life is a handout, something for nothing.' If *that's* the truth, he sure need to be glad, because that was how he got rich off poor, black people, running his get-rich-easy cons on them.

"My mother said in them early days, it looked like wasn't nothing your father could do to make the people fall out of love with him. It was like he was charmed. He went right to the top of the religion business with his Church of the Divine Investigation, opening a big church here in Newark, then doing the same thing in New York, Philly, Chicago, on and on like that. Newark Police Department made him an honorary member of the force. I remember how when I was a girl the white men was always throwing appreciation banquets for him at the Robert Treat Hotel.

"But as far as I'm concerned Sam Poole was only one thing—a pimp. And every pimp, even if he had all the women Sam Poole had, always has one woman what inspired him and put him out there in the first place. All his women after her don't be nothing but a stand-in for her model. I always thought I would like to have seen the woman meant all that to Daddy Poole. I can't never see her, but at least I know who she was: that Jewel of Newark, the one you say he call Mozelle. I heard about her, but I never put it together till today. She was a conjurer, so I heard when I was coming up, and if your father know anything about that mess, she was the one taught him. She went to Montmartre, and he used to go there too. He was visiting her, I guess, till she died. She was the power behind the power. I never believed much in hoodoo, but I know them what practice it believe you got to keep power *in* something—a doll, a hank of hair, a bottle—could be anything. *She* give him something. That's where his power come from. If you could find it, you'd have Daddy by his balls. I wonder what it is."

Martha swung around and faced Peanut, ready to speak. She caught herself in time. All she said was, "I better be getting cross the way. I still got to pick up Man."

"Why don't you let that baby-sitter keep him for another night. I'm fixing to call Archie and let him know not to meet me at the bar tonight. He be off work in a couple of hours. I'm going to have him take me over to Brooklyn. Aint no use trying to party in Newark. You know some loud nigger'll tell Pete they seen me, and I'm supposed to be sick. Come on with us. You need to get out and dance. Do you good to let go. We a *dancing, muscle-working* people."

"I can't remember the last time I danced or heard something to make me feel like I want to dance. I got to get over there and see about my father. I hung out long enough. Thanks for the beer. Tell Archie I said hey. Take it easy."

Patti and Iphigenia took the key from behind the gravy pitcher in the china cabinet and went upstairs, laughing and eating red Pixy Stix. They unlocked the door to their mother's bedroom and went inside. They had never known their mother to share a bedroom with Jimmy Anderson. Patti jumped on the pink satin bedspread and struck a movie-star pose. Iphigenia turned on the stereo. She searched the stacks of records along the wall. Patti reached across the bed and took a bottle of Shalimar perfume from the nightstand. Iphigenia turned, holding a scratched record. "You better not mess up Mama's bed."

"She won't know the difference."

She looked into Patti's smoke-gray eyes. "You heard what I said, didn't you?" Iphigenia let the needle drop on the turning record. In a moment the room filled with Billie Holiday singing "My Man." Iphigenia shaped her lips, as she imagined the singer would, swaying in her mother's big dress.

Patti watched in jealousy and awe. "What you know about a man?" demanded Patti, sitting up on the bed, dabbing her earlobes with perfume. "Who is 'your man'?"

Iphigenia waited until the song was finished before she answered, "Sam Poole."

Sister Sarah was still on the porch. Jimmy Anderson was working the swing shift, four o'clock to midnight. Those overheated and tired children were still in the street, making noise. Now it was a game of jump rope.

> *In comes the doctor.*
> *In comes the nurse.*
> *In comes the lady with*
> *The alligator purse.*
>
> *Teddy Bear, Teddy Bear,*
> *Turn around.*
> *Teddy Bear, Teddy Bear,*
> *Touch the ground.*

Out goes the cat.
Out goes the rat.
Out goes the lady with
The big ball hat.

The children came from every direction to play. They jumped the rope three at a time. They jumped Double Dutch. They jumped into the rope, leaping to the beat, twisting and shouting. They touched the ground. They put their hands on their hips. Their arms reached and stretched. They took turns turning the rope. When one of them missed and got tangled in the rope, the turners pulled the rope taut.

Sister Anderson got up and went to the screen door. "You children," she called, her mouth at the dusty screen. "Do you hear me?" She called until there was not silence on the street but something remarkably close to it. The children, several stone steps below her, stopped playing and turned around in a perfect rectangle.

"You children," she continued, "have played outside my door all afternoon. Now I'm sick of it. If you don't have a home to go to, then just get away from mine."

They began to run.

"And if I ever catch one of you sitting out in front of this door, I'll take a pot of scalding water and pour it right down these steps," she added, her heart beating fast.

Sister Anderson had finally struck the chord she wanted. All day those children had penetrated her thoughts with their wild ruckus. Now they were gone. Prince Street grew dark and quiet. There was, miraculously, no automobile or bus moving in the street. Even the calls of birds were arrested by some soothing power. Now she thought of old times. Sarah stood at the screen and looked up into the sky, a vast, flipped-over bowl in which starry lights were coming on.

Then she saw Martha Poole walking down the street with the

baby in her arms. Martha moved like an old woman in disguise, the motherless child becoming the mother of black Newark, her shoulders hunched forward with Man as though trying to protect an exposed, bleeding heart. Her maid's uniform had lost the freshness and shine it possessed that morning when Sister Sarah watched her leave number 28. Martha walked slowly and heavily as if each step were a prayer for assistance.

That morning, Martha had taken the bus for the long ride out to Belleville, where she had spent the day serving. Then she rode back to Newark and had the senseless fight with Peanut (Peanut could talk more shit than the TV set) and picked up Man from the baby-sitter, who cursed her as usual for being late. Now she pulled her weight down Prince Street and dragged herself into number 28.

8.

～～ "Must Jesus bear the cross alone?" the minister's voice rolled toward a crescendo. "Must Jesus bear the cross alone, and all the world go free? No, there's a cross for everyone, and there's a cross for me. All Wise and Mighty Everlasting God, Our Heavenly Father, it is once more again, Lord, that your servant is bowing down here before You."

In the summer of 1945, Poole's Newark congregation visited the Temple of the Most Precious Blood in Queens, New York, for the Revival Day service. *It is once more again, Lord.* Rows of ginger-colored women tilted their heads, casting their faces into the shadows of bold hats, and said, "Do, Lord." The men moaned.

The storefront church was on a long boulevard of dead houses standing up against each other. A sabbatic stillness was in the air.

One flight above the church, in her tenement room, a woman awoke to find her man gone. Her mink coat was missing from its hanger over the bed. The two hundred dollars she had been saving to go to Chicago was gone from the pillowcase. She looked at the clock. Noon. She reached under the rag bed and took out her cigarettes. She rose on her elbows to verify all that she suspected. She crossed the room to turn on the electric fan, and then she could hear the streetcar, way in the distance, starting up the narrow boulevard. *Must Jesus . . . Do, Lord.*

In the church, the people stood up against each other like houses. They stood against the doors and walls and filled the pews. Everyone looked toward Daddy standing in the pulpit. Everyone was listening to his prayer. His voice rolled through the static pools of sunlight that came down through the high windows. The church listened, and the woman, in her room upstairs, inhaling her cigarette deeply, listened too. Her mind seized upon his voice as if it were the last voice left living on earth: *Must Jesus bear the cross alone?*

Daddy Poole sat on a stepped throne chair enclosed by brass handrails. He sat on the third level and rested his feet on the second level. Only Poole sat in this seat, because he was the one whom God had sent. To his followers, this seat was the Throne of Grace. The structure of the seat was made of wood and could be collapsed and reassembled wherever he preached. The structure had been built to Poole's specifications. Only Poole knew the significance of the seat. Everyone else projected a personal meaning onto the wooden throne and onto Daddy Poole when he took his seat on its topmost level.

He wore a shining white robe. The perspiration on his brow made a glistening mosaic. A placard on the wall beside the altar read: IT CAN BE DONE. Broken canes and crutches were heaped at the foot of the altar.

The ceiling fans revolved slowly.

The streetcar stopped at the corner in front of the church at last. It had been on its way forever. No one boarded. It moved on. Poole waited until the sound of the streetcar was dead.

"Lord, You know my heart, and You know my mind. If there be any sin lurking in my heart, pluck it out and cast it into the sea of forgetfulness where it will never again rise to condemn me in this world or the next."

The women churned pleated paper fans.

"Let us say amen." He was no longer speaking to God, but to the congregation. He looked down, searching their faces. Some of them looked away.

The people said amen.

"Let the church say amen. Let us say amen again. Lift your hand and say, 'Thank you, Jesus. Thank you, Jesus. Thank you, Jesus.' The Lord is good and worthy to be praised. The Lord said if He be lifted up He would draw all men unto Him. I praise Him this afternoon. I give honor to God, the clergy of Most Precious Blood, saints, friends. . . . I count it a privilege to bring His word one more time. I thank Him for how He has healed my spiritual and physical life.

"Those of you who have your Bible may turn now to Matthew, the twenty-fifth chapter, beginning with the first verse."

The church people turned the leaves of the scripture. Ushers, dressed in red and white to symbolize the Purity and the Love, dispensed Bibles through the temple. Those elders of the church, who could not read but were as familiar with the gospel as they were with the lines in the palms of their own hands, believed they knew the word Poole was going to bring.

Daddy did not need a Bible. He had the whole text of God memorized. He even knew the portion of the Bible God had commanded his apostle to seal up until the end of time.

"Then," said the preacher, *"shall the kingdom of heaven be likened unto ten virgins, which took their lamps, and went forth to meet the bridegroom. And five of them were wise, and five were foolish. They that were foolish took their lamps and took no oil with them. But the wise took oil in their vessels with their lamps. While the bridegroom tarried, they all slumbered and slept."*

In his left hand, Daddy held a pure gold staff, a hoodoo stick from Egypt. The stick was invisible to anyone but Daddy Poole. He described the staff as a living rod with a triple cross at the top and a crystal at the bottom the size of a pool cube.

"And at midnight there was a cry made, Behold, the bridegroom cometh; go ye out to meet him. Then all those virgins arose, and trimmed their lamps. And the foolish said unto the wise, Give us of your oil; for our lamps are gone out."

Poole and the assembly read, recited, droned together.

"But the wise answered, saying, Not so; less there be not enough for us and you: but go ye rather to them that sell, and buy for yourselves. And while they went to buy, the bridegroom came; and they that were ready went in with him to the marriage: and the door was shut."

Daddy raised and lowered his right hand three times. He wore a visible crown patterned with inlaid pieces of gems in the frame.

"I want to take my text," he said, "from the sixth verse: *And at midnight there was a cry made, Behold, the bridegroom cometh.*"

He went into a trance.

"Early one of these mornings," he said, "and it won't be much longer now . . ."

"Break it down, preacher."

"Make it real."

"Yes. Tell it."

". . . you're going to look for me, but I'll be gone. I don't know the day, the hour. But one day . . . one day, when Gabriel's trumpet sounds deep in my soul, I'm going to cash in my cross for a crown. It's going to be way late some evening, early one of these mornings, and it won't be long, Jesus is going to come."

"Hallelujah."

"He's going to dispel heartaches, vanquish sickness and sorrow in that midnight hour. At midnight we can shout our troubles over, for the King of Kings and the Lord of Lords is going to come back and carry us home.

"I feel He's soon to come. Every day I'm living to live again. Every day I'm watching for His return. The end of this world is at hand. God is fixing to shake the world. It's three minutes to midnight on the great clock."

His head fell forward with a sudden jerk. His crown fell down the throne. It was retrieved by an attendant.

"The Bible tells us that in that day there will be wars and the rumor of wars. We will hear of wars and commotion. Some will quit the faith and give heed to seducing spirits and the doctrines of devils. Then God will shake the world. He's going to shake off the incontinent . . ."

"Yeah, yeah."

". . . the incontinent and proud. Shake off the unholy and murderous. The world is going to twist and retch. The Bible tells us that in that Day of Days there's going to be two in the bed. One's going to be taken and the other left. There's going to be two in the field. One's going to be taken, and the other's going to be left. There's going to be two grinding at the mill. One's going to be taken and the other's going to be left. Heaven and earth will pass with a great noise. The elements are going to melt with a fervent heat. The earth and all our works will be burned up."

The women compressed their legs together. The men sweated.

"At midnight when He comes back, He's coming back for a church without a spot or a wrinkle. You may think He's coming back for a building, but not so. You will find that the bride, when she marches down the aisle, is dressed in a beautiful white gown, and there're no spots and there're no wrinkles on that gown. And when He comes, Beloved, there can't be any spots or wrinkles in our lives."

"Yes. Make it real!"

"We who are in the faith, we have to stay ready because we don't know the day or the hour the bridegroom is coming. We have to guard every aspect of our lives. We have to keep our lamps burning because the signs of his soon coming are everywhere. Times are waxing hard in the land. The soil won't yield the way it used to yield. Our nation is nothing but clay and brass and iron. People are sold like cigarettes. Men's hearts are hardening, and now we can see the Son of Man is soon to come. You may be in the church when He comes, jumping and singing and shouting. You may be turning in your bed, asleep—Daddy doesn't know, the point is this: We have to stay ready—ready for the Rapture to take place.

"When He comes and spreads His throne in the middle of the air . . . the Creator of the World is going to sneak up behind us. He's going to take up the instrument of his mental power. He's going to strike the still space and lay it open with a gash—opening a new world, a new Jerusalem where the streets are made of gold and the gates of pearl. In His crown, He'll be wearing the morning stars."

Foam formed at the sides of his mouth. "I see the holy city this afternoon and the new Jerusalem coming down from heaven, prepared as a bride for her husband. The Rapture is just about to take place. Get your oil. Get your lamp. It's almost midnight. The cry is about to be made. The Rapture is just about to take place. Are you ready? When two men working in a field will become one. When the redeemed of the Lord go marching in and sit down together in Glory around His sanctified throne and praise His name forever. It's almost midnight. It's almost midnight. It's almost—" shouted the preacher.

"Midnight!"

"It's almost—"

"Midnight!"

"It's almost midnight; it's almost midnight; it's almost midnight! It's almost—"

Holy ghost-fire poured over the place. The choir stood in a festooned choir box and sang "There Is a Fountain Filled with Blood." The spirit of the hymn rocked the house to a steady beat. The sisters danced under the annointing. The men spoke in tongue. The children drummed their hands and feet and rolled the tambourines.

The woman upstairs had listened to each word of the sermon. When the music started she rose again and put makeup on her legs, face and arms. The woman was Sarah Anderson. It was not easy for Sarah to see the woman of 1945 as herself, not easy for her to claim that sinking woman whom Daddy's voice, rising from the bottom of the building like a universal flood, had saved. He had drawn her out of many waters that day and carried her into a large place. The spiritless, high-toned girl was she. Yes. The way the girl wore her hair with flattened side curls and the crown heavily slicked on the top of one side was the way Sarah had worn her hair then. Now when Sister Sarah looked back down the years from her screened porch in Newark, she could scarcely see the Queens tenement room, and the girl was transparent to the point of disappearing. Sarah moved across the shadowy porch, following the ghost of herself.

It had been she. She had fought with her young husband, Jimmy Anderson. She had left him, strapped her savings to her thigh and taken her mink coat. She ran away to New York City and went straight to Harlem. She was at a cabaret called the Mad House when she met a man. He was a gambler and small-time con artist. He persuaded her to move in with him in his room in Queens. His teeth shone like a diamond amulet against suspicion. She could not remember his face, his body or his name. She remembered how he filled the tiny room at night, making love to her body. She remembered the unwieldy silence he left in his wake. Had she been making love to herself all along, fooling herself? She awoke and found herself alone. She could not feel anything until she heard the preacher's voice from downstairs. His voice lapped at her feet. She had dressed herself under the power of the sermon. The echoes of the preacher's voice stayed close behind her as she threw clothes into her bag and descended the building to the street.

A small whirlpool of air stirred on the boulevard. Sarah stood an infinite moment on the street, not knowing where to place her feet. She mused on the windows of the stacked-up houses. She wondered at all the people who might be hidden behind those windows. She watched the windows fill up with the faces of an imagined multitude, frozen, because the spirit of God had settled on the world. They wanted to run, but there was no-where to run. They wanted to hide, but there was no hiding place. So they waited.

She was still standing on the street when Daddy Poole emerged from the church, encircled by his flock.

"Daddy, but you preached this afternoon. Did my soul good."

"Lord, didn't we have a *time*."

"We been trying to get you down in Maryland since February, Daddy."

"Daddy, you got to come and preach that for us in Detroit."

"God bless your stout soul, Daddy."

Sarah had not realized it was Poole's voice she heard from upstairs, but when she saw him come out of the church something fell in place inside her. It could have been no one else. She had been living in the house across from his in Newark for about a year. He was a brown mountain of a man with a miracle of a voice. He looked as if all he had to do was open his mouth for Heaven to darken and the earth to shake. She had heard his gospel program on the radio in Newark. He came on the radio late Sunday nights. She had seen him at her mother's restaurant.

"Do you know him?" she asked her mother, leaning on the cool lunch counter.

Savannah Sparks was at the cash register near her daughter's head. The question seemed to aggravate her. "I know him." She fixed him with a cruel gaze across the room.

"Who is he?"

"You act like you want him."

"What if I do, Mama?" She had not met Jimmy Anderson then. She was not long from the South. Savannah Sparks had given birth to Sarah in Newark, but the girl was raised in Georgia where Savannah was raised. Savannah rented rooms on Hillside Place and ran the Old Mali Restaurant on Boston Street. The restaurant was known for her fried chicken and homemade sweet potato pies.

"Then you're a damn fool. That preacher's got too many women to suit me."

Sarah sat up and turned to look at him through the crowded restaurant. He was more than a man. He was living food. His greased-back hair, just beginning to silver at the edges, was as rich as the vegetation of Beulah. She kept her voice close to her mother. "Church folks don't have to do what a preacher does," she said philosophically. "If they're aiming for the Kingdom," she parried, "all they have to do is what he says."

She had been a forthright, careless girl and passionate about men. She went to men for help. When they fought she got another man. Her face, her hair, her walk constituted a question which men, seeing, answered. When she married, her husband was away much of the time, driving long-distance. He had his other women here and there. She felt her body had used her and dragged her over a low way. She had already begun to pray, but she knew these prayers never rose beyond the rooms in which they were prayed. She had what the saints down South called a double heart. She was living a divided existence, her soul wrestling with her body, her mind yearning for the final marriage.

Sister Anderson met God in 1938. As a child she lay before the altar of a Georgia church house, stricken by the blast from

God's mighty nostrils. She came to consciousness with her face on the floor. Everyone said that God had saved her, had become her living and breathing and had given her the Holy Ghost, a god at hand. She had walked uprightly for a time, but as she grew she burned in her bed clothes night after night, waking to red dreams of the North, where her mother, whom she barely knew then, lived a life Sarah's Southern aunt had been too holy to describe. She told herself stories in which glamorous men gave her furs and earrings that clung at her ears like beads of blood. If she was to come to God, she would need a man to carry her the distance.

Daddy Poole was Sarah's man. There was not a doubt in her mind. When he passed her in front of the Temple of the Most Precious Blood in 1945, she followed him, and when he recognized her as his neighbor from Newark, she took the seat beside him in the back of his car and, without a word, rode.

9.

≈≈≈ _M_artha let herself into 28 and toiled up the steps to the second floor. She let Man crawl up the stairs behind her. Before entering the apartment, she stared at the door, anxious and interested. She listened. She heard nothing. She sighed and went in.

There were stains at her feet where blood had dyed the carpet. It was only blood from the white chicken she killed last night hoping to restore her father's health. She had rode the bus out to Somerset County and back for that chicken. The damned thing ran all over the apartment when she bit into its jugular vein.

The apartment was small and heaped with a multitude of objects. There was an altar in the northeast corner of the front room piled with pictures of Catholic saints, bottles of Coca-Cola and cigars. Martha's bed was next to the altar. Most of the chairs in the room were broken. Two stuffed chairs, without legs, were propped against the wall near the front door. Quantities of dead flowers hung on the wall. The edges of the room and beneath the altar were cluttered with bound stacks of newspapers going back to 1964. A Bible that had been "visited" by the Spirit lay on the altar.

Martha had taken the chicken by the wing last night and cleaned out its guts over the kitchen sink. She filled its chest with cornmeal and pepper and placed it at the altar in a bowl. She crossed two candles with a knife and tied them with yellow and white ribbons. She laid them at the altar. On one side of the bowl she placed opened bottles of Coca-Cola, and on the other side, bunches of cigars tied with ribbons. She placed a box of matches in front of the cigars.

Daddy had taught her these things too late in his life, and Martha's magic always failed. Her father had been notorious for his conjures during the thirties and forties. Behind the front of his church ministry, he had sold high-priced remedies and "fixes" to everyone from purse snatchers to mayors. People in Newark once believed Daddy Poole could kill or resurrect life by remote control.

Martha had wrapped the dead chicken in newspaper and put it out with the trash that morning.

She traveled the room slowly and paused at the door to the bedroom. Man made a sound, startling her. She looked down. He wanted to be picked up.

The first thing she noticed when she entered his room was the snakehide hanging above his bed. It had hung there so long she had stopped seeing it until now. Daddy was asleep with his mouth open. His hands clutched the covers to his chin. The candle she had lighted in the morning was still burning. Martha went into silence and talked to the Spirit through the candle.

Sister Sarah came in from her porch. She stopped inside the vestibule, studying herself in the mirror. The time was soon now to serve dinner. Patti and Iphigenia were upstairs running the water for their baths.

Sarah's reflection in the mirror pleased her. At fifty-five, her beauty looked inexhaustible. Her skin was still smooth. Her face was a miracle of ovals and soft ellipses. Her eyes had the same black mystery as a new moon. Something necessary had been robbed from those eyes long ago, but the theft was belied by the glittering blackness. Her eyes told none of her secrets.

On the left side of her face she had a tiny mole like a black crescent, dripping down the corner of her mouth. Daddy Poole had called this her beauty mark. Beauty had marked her here, he said, leaving behind a signature on its work. Sarah washed her face twice a day with the juice from a cucumber and a lime. Each week she steeped special herbs for her hair and skin. She wore her hair bound in a tall pompadour.

There were mirrors in every room of her house. Her mother believed mirrors protected one from the gaze of evil spirits. Savannah had ordered six hundred dollars' worth of mirrors from Bamberger department store and gave them to her daughter and son-in-law as a wedding gift. She instructed Sarah that ghosts were embarrassed by mirrors since ghosts have no reflection. Sister Sarah was not afraid of ghosts. She installed the mirrors because, being naturally vain, she enjoyed watching herself in every room.

She had lived in the house for so long and spent so much time alone with its rooms and mirrors that she had become troubled and restless. She had begun to lose her mind.

Sarah Anderson's mind was taking her backward like a reversed train car, traveling back through what was already past. It was odd the way mirrors reversed things. Doors that had opened right to left were now opening left to right. Her right hand became her left, and the tiny mole dripped from the left side of her mouth. Sister Sarah knew she was crazy, but she had begun to enjoy the lulling motion of going backward, of going farther and farther back to some tremendous event. Her mind was playing a trick on her, and instead of distressing her, the trick amused Sarah. She had stopped resisting what was happening to her mind. Senility would be another weapon against what was real, like her isolation, the television set and her doctor's prescriptions.

She went nowhere that was not related to church or buying food. She saw no one except bill collectors, and these she handled with perfunctory coldness. She was always alone in the house. While Jimmy was gone and the girls were at school, even when her family was somewhere in the house saying something or moving, Sarah always felt alone. The Spartan solitude she had practiced for so many years failed her now. In her sleeping dreams and in her waking dreams her mind raced her backward and, with a clarity that held her for whole hours, she relived the past.

"Mama," cried Iphigenia from the second floor, "Patti won't stop running the water and take her bath."

"The water is too hot, Mama," Patti whined.

"The water is *not* too hot," Iphigenia said. "I tested it with my elbow. She just don't want to take her bath."

Sister Sarah did not move. Her unraised voice reached the second story of the house with chilling accuracy: "Patti, get into the tub, dear."

She went into the living room and looked at a magazine. She refilled the offertory bowl of peppermint balls and smoothed the gossamer drapes in front of the windows. On top of the television set there were pictures of her children: the girls and her grown son living in Los Angeles. The mirror was over the mantel. She kept a picture of Daddy on the mantelpiece beside a white French clock.

Poole had been her man for nine years.

She had lived with him all over the world. He schooled her in his ways and presided at her initiation ceremonies into his church. She was his protégée, his secretary, his girlfriend, his hostess. Visitors to his Broome Street church soon came for a glimpse of Sister Sarah as well as to hear and see the inimitable Daddy Poole. The light from the Art Deco chandeliers hanging from the ceiling exuded majesty and magic. She would be there moving through that light, wearing the costumes Daddy bought her from fashion houses in Paris and London. She put on her best diction and displayed fine manners. She was well dressed. Her hair was always smoothly arranged, sometimes with intricate hairpieces like those worn by the negro women entertainers, and held with ornaments made of rhino horn and ivory.

She was baptized in a wading pool built into the back wall of the church's pulpit. A giant panel depicting the Last Supper slid back to reveal the pool. Daddy baptized nearly a hundred people that day. Then the panel closed and Poole preached a sermon that "shouted" the entire congregation.

Daddy had helped reconcile her marriage and then had taken her as his own woman. Jimmy Anderson and Daddy became friends. The men were fishing partners for many years. Jimmy drove the truck for Daddy's used-furniture company in Orange. Jimmy escorted Sarah to the parties Daddy had in number 28. The two men loved each other. In some way Sarah could not tell, Daddy possessed Jimmy as fully as he had been able to possess her those nine years. For nine years, Daddy was spiritually married to both husband and wife.

Sarah and Daddy fucked and worked together. They got drunk and played bid whist, tonk and pitty pat on trains. They had an apartment in New York in the West Seventies. She drew out eminent people at parties and introduced them to Sam Poole. He introduced her to famous racketeers and jazz musicians. He took her to the mob-owned nightclubs.

She was the ornament of Daddy's organization during the nine years he was at the top of his game. She spoke for him with the press. They went regularly to the Joe Louis Bar. Sometimes they fell by Minton's Playhouse down the street from the Apollo. She still had her bebop records locked in her bedroom upstairs. They went to the bright, white supper parties downtown. They rode airliners and ships and big automobiles.

In Milan, Daddy introduced her to prosciutto and melon. She wore a marquisette gown to a fund-raising dinner in Lyons, dragging an ermine and foxtail sweep. She wore a weightless dress of ostrich plumes to a political reception in Zanzibar.

In Zanzibar he pretended to marry her. Then they were settled in the Niger while Daddy established his African missions. He gave her a second initiation there. She purified herself for seven days, fasting and praying. For seven nights he did not have sex with her. He brought bathing pots to her tent in the mornings and bathed her with infusions made from barks and leaves. He dried her with printed fabrics and blew cigar smoke over her. At night he fanned her in her tent and talked to her about the beginning of the world and the sacred predators who had come from the sky. He taught her about the spirits inside candles, how to move things through the spirits of candles by lighting them and pinching them out. Finally he baptized her again, this time in the redolent River Niger. When she came up from the water, he said she was a mystery as old as the stars.

They spent a year between Onitsha and Benin City. She wanted to go back to Paris or Spain, even Harlem. Daddy claimed he needed her there. For what? To sit around the house playing solitaire, smoking hand-rolled cigarettes? All the house servants called her Ezenwanyi, meaning Queen of All Women. She sensed though that the African women were suspicious of her. She was suspicious of herself. She had no sense of being a sister to these common women. Whatever bond there was between herself and them had withered in the ages. Daddy was often gone on long business trips. She was certain he now had other women. He would return with blueprints and plans for new religious centers. He wanted to build mission boats to move along the continent. He poured talk of African wealth. He spoke endlessly of unexploited copper, zinc, manganese and, in the Congo, uranium. Occasionally there were small dinner parties for American and European enterprisers. Business was discussed at these parties. Daddy expected her to excuse herself before dessert.

She felt disgusted with herself when she complained. She had chosen to be with Daddy. It was not like being with Jimmy Anderson. It was not like seeing Jimmy now and then, going in and out, knowing he had different women. The difference was that Daddy was a happy man. Jimmy Anderson had chosen her. She had chosen Daddy. She smiled just thinking of how handsome Daddy was in Africa, how fat and happy he grew.

She made the best of things. She learned to shoot a rifle. She even went hunting once and shot a gazelle. She refused to eat any of the animal. For a while she owned a tame owl that rested on her shoulder in the evenings. Once a week a servant drove her to Agbor in a silver jeep. While he gathered food, gasoline and sundries at the trading post there, Sarah chatted with a shop owner's wife, an encompassing Ibo lady with a huge gap in her front teeth. Sarah never saw the woman get up from the rocking chair at the back of the stall or remove the clay pipe she kept tight in her fingers. When Sarah came around, Redempta Agbim ordered one of her grown children to bring out another rocking chair and a plate of dried fish. The two women talked and rocked in their chairs. They had no fear of one another. The rocking of the chairs sounded like laughing and talking.

Redempta had been a bride at age eleven. She was a rebellious wife in the beginning. When her husband went to work with the men, she had sought out boyfriends among the younger boys. Now she was a grandmother. She held the Christian missionaries from Britain and the United States in great esteem and went by the name given her by a white mission woman. She had heard of Daddy Poole and said it was due to his presense that the river had come back after a three-year drought and the locusts stayed away. She wore high, colorful turbans and very little jewelry. Her husband was now ill, and her sons managed the store. Often the Ibo woman had Vichy water and French perfume. Sarah had the servant buy these things also.

"I must have told that old woman everything I experienced in life," Sarah said to no one, fingering the mantel in the living room. "She could listen to me for hours like I was speaking her own mind. Listening is an art and not everybody has it. Redempta was the best company I ever had next to Daddy. I believed I was barren, but she told me that Daddy would give me a child. She had that much faith in his miracles. I tried to explain to her that I stopped bleeding when I was nineteen years old. You'll embrace a son, she kept telling me, and I laughed in that old woman's face. She said, 'What about Sarah in the Bible who bore a baby with Abraham when she was old *and* barren? And the Shunammite woman? Nothing is too hard for God.'

"She was right. Redempta was right. But she was wrong about Daddy. Daddy wasn't my baby's father. He wasn't. Mama said Emmett looked just like Daddy, but that's only because I favor Daddy myself in looks. She tried to say Patti and Iphigenia look like Daddy. I told her she was crazy. I told her to stop insinuating lies about my babies. 'I'm their mother,' I said. 'Don't I know the father of my own children?!'"

Sarah thought she heard someone call her. She turned around and answered, "Yes?"

Patti and Iphigenia were coming down the stairs slowly with their hands on the banister. They had on matching pajamas and bedroom slippers.

Iphigenia said, "We didn't call you, Mama."

Patti said matter-of-factly to Iphigenia, "She thought she heard somebody calling her again."

Iphigenia hushed her sister. She said, "We took our baths, Mama. Can we watch television before dinner?"

"No. I want you to go back to your room and play with your dolls until suppertime."

The girls turned around on the stairs.

Sarah went into the kitchen and swept the floor, forgetting to feel the broom in her hands. As she swept, her mind fell on her last return to Newark with Daddy Poole. She returned to Newark Airport with him many times from Africa, South America, Russia. This had been the last time, and she had not been out of Newark since. There was a parade starting at the seated Lincoln statue at the Court House, up Springfield Avenue to Belmont Avenue. The women of the Metaphysical Church of the Divine Investigation—they all called themselves virgins—marched behind a drum and bugle corps. The virgins wore red and white, waving flags and holding signs. Daddy and Sarah followed the women in the procession, riding in a garlanded parade car. In the presence of hundreds of Daddy's people, Sarah was still the most striking member of his entourage.

That was the end of her time with Poole. Their time had passed like an era. Daddy had wanted to use her as a priestess for his church. He wanted to take away her sexuality. He wanted her to practice celibacy while he had sex with other women. She refused. She went back to Jimmy Anderson and maintaining a home. Daddy got Jimmy a truck-driving job with a large company in Harrison, New Jersey. Sarah attended the Pentecostal Church on Prince Street, where she was a member of the Burial Society. She, along with several other married women, folded her hair in an immaculate bonnet and put on a long black dress to make up the beds of the dead. In recent times this particular function had become diminished since most deaths occurred in hospitals. She was called to no more than one or two deaths each year. These were, as it happened, the deaths most precious to the congregation, being usually those of the very elderly or of infants.

She realized her travels with Daddy were, more than a journey in space, a journey in time. That time was as consuming as a dream reaching out, forever calling her name.

Sister Sarah washed her hands in the kitchen sink. Then she sliced a loaf of bread and put it in a wicker basket. She placed the dishes and silverware on the table, moving the objects without a sound. She was serving fish gumbo the way Daddy liked it.

Martha's luck was no good. She had tried everything, and everything had failed. Her father smelled more like death each day. His doctors had given him up. The money in his savings accounts was gone. If he had any more money, Martha did not know about it. City Hospital said there was no point in admitting him anymore. He acted proud. He said he wanted to die at home in his own bed. A score of root doctors, psychic readers and healers had been in and out of the house during the summer to stand over his bed and pronounce the same verdict. She was warned not to hope. The judgment on her father was death. Martha did not care what people said. Her father was God. That was all she knew.

She got up from her knees and pinched out the candle.

Martha went to the front room and changed Man's diaper. He probably had not slept all day. He was a good baby, never cried unless something scared him. He was fat, and his hands were big. He was going to be a giant, like his grandfather. There was nothing wrong with her baby, Martha told herself: Peanut was wrong. She nursed him and laid him along her shoulder, patting his smooth back. She put him on the cot and surrounded him with pillows. She stayed and watched him.

His tiny hands were always reaching up, even in his sleep, to take hold of the world. It was a sign he was going to be—he had to be—somebody—a *man*. He was going to grow up to do things and know people, sport nice clothes and drive a large car. He was so much man, she had hardly been able to carry him for nine months. He was going to be too much man for one woman. He would have plenty of women and always have money. Man would find a way out of this maze of streets. He would come back too—and lead his mother out.

In the kitchen, Martha crushed garlic with coffee and sugar. She put a little of the mixture into a censer and lit it, walking through the apartment. As she walked she said the Twenty-third Psalm.

The telephone rang when she came back into the kitchen. It was Reverend Leon. He was at the Greyhound bus station downtown. He wanted to know which bus to take to Prince Street. Martha had cashed her welfare check last week and sent all $436 to Reverend Leon in Harter, Mississippi.

She told him to go around to Pennsylvania Station, catch the number 9 bus and get off on South Orange Avenue. Or he could get the number 25 to Prince Street and Springfield Avenue and walk toward South Orange Avenue.

He said, "I hope we be able to remember all that, Sister Martha. It's so many cars and people in the streets."

"Who is 'we'?" Martha asked. "You never said nothing about no damn 'we.'"

"I got my wife and mother-in-law with me."

There was a pause. "Well, maybe you should get a taxi, Reverend Leon."

"All I can afford is a bus. Our traveling expense was so high. I had to make up the cure for your father special, and the ingredients cost me a lot of other money besides."

"All right then, just get a cab and tell the driver where to let you off. I'll pay for the cab when you get here."

"Bless you, Sister Martha. I'll be there directly. Good-bye."

"'Bye." Martha hung up and took her last ten-dollar bill from between her breasts. She went downstairs to wait for the preacher.

She had never met Reverend Leon. He had first called her on

the phone a month ago. She still didn't know how he had gotten her phone number. He called all the way from Mississippi to tell her that he had seen her in a vision. He said the trees behind his shack had spoken to him, telling him to heal her father. The vision told him exactly how the healing was to be performed. It would be difficult to snatch a powerful man like Daddy, against his will, from death, but Reverend Leon claimed to be the man for the job. He guaranteed satisfaction for five hundred dollars in advance and five hundred dollars when the results were achieved. He claimed to have something special. Something that made him the most powerful healer in the South. She asked him what he had, but he would not tell her over the phone.

The cab pulled up to the curb after a while. Martha was sitting on the stoop smoking a Kool cigarette. Reverend Leon stepped from the cab first and got the money from Martha. He went back, paid the fare and helped two women carrying luggage to the curb. The taxi drove on with the driver yelling, "Cheap countrified motherfuckers."

The women wore printed summer dresses and had on auburn long-haired wigs that came down to their waists. They were both young women. They were about the same purple-black complexion. They had pretty figures and long arms. That their teeth should be so straight and dazzling white surprised Martha. The women shone in the dreary streetlight as though their skin had been rubbed with butter. Even their faces.

The travelers approached the stoop. The reverend had taken the luggage. There were three broken suitcases tied with thick rope.

Reverend Leon grinned and spoke. "Praise God. Here is we, Sister Martha. Praise God. This here is Lottie, my wife, and Sister Inez—I hates to say mother-in-law—my mother."

Martha narrowed her eyes and sucked her teeth. "Sister Inez, you look awful young to be a grown man's mother."

Sister Inez tried to blush.

Reverend Leon jumped in. He was a little man with a porkpie hat stuck on the back of his head. He looked like someone had slapped his head around to give him that crooked neck. "Sis Inez pretty used to people saying she look like Lottie's sister. Plenty of us done things before coming to God that we had to seek forgiveness for. Sister Inez give birth to Lottie when she wasn't nothing but twelve years old."

The women said nothing.

Martha said, "Where's my change from the cab?"

He set the suitcases down and gave Martha five dollars and some change.

Martha stood and wiped the back of her dress with her hands. "Come on. I'll show you where Daddy is at." Reverend Leon took one of the suitcases and told Lottie and Inez to stay downstairs with the luggage.

"Now, I just want you to show me where he is," he said, as Martha led him up the stairs in the hall. "Then I want you to come back down and talk with the women. I won't be long. I got to be alone with my patient when I perform my work."

"Well, he aint clean. I got to change him. I aint been too long from work, and he got shit on him."

10.

"I'm going to dance that holy dance . . ."
—SONG

〰〰 *M*artha sat in the dark living room holding her baby's hand, watching him sleep. Reverend Leon was younger than she had expected. He did not look more than thirty-five years old. He was ugly enough to have a strange power. Bug eyes and raw-looking liver lips covered with a moustache. His voice sounded like a door swinging on rusted hinges. He smelled about as bad as Daddy. Martha could not stand a young man who would not wash and keep himself clean. Even if a man was ugly, he could still respect his body with soap and water. Well, Reverend Leon could not make Daddy any worse, she thought, and she was not paying him for his looks.

Reverend Leon untied his suitcase and lifted the top. He took out a surgical knife and cut open four of the sores on Daddy's chest. He put honey inside the incisions, then rum, then bright, black Mississippi leeches. He looked down with a sweet, sick smile at the man whose legend he had heard throughout his childhood. He looked at what remained of the man who had flown up from a burning house into an immortal night, leaving the generations in Harter to tell their children.

"You don't look like too much of nothing now, do you? Don't worry none, old man, you got folks in Harter still believe in you. I believe in you, baby. You has walked and talked with me every day of my life. Help me a little bit now won't you? We going to show your little girl a wonder."

As if by signal of fear, Martha burst into the room. She looked at the bed and screamed.

Daddy awoke and looked at himself. He stretched his mouth but did not make a sound.

Martha pulled the leeches from him, bursting them with her fingernails. Reverend Leon tried to stop her. "Get out of here! You don't know what you doing!"

Martha turned on him and slapped his mouth several times before he could grab her hands. She spit in his face.

He looked at her, shocked. "You crazy?"

She twisted her hands. "You trying to kill him, motherfucker. You used me. You aint shit. You used me for a free ride north."

He threw her against the bed and started packing his suitcase. "Stupid bitch. I was the last chance he had."

Martha leaped to the floor and bit his leg through his trousers. She tasted his blood. She hollered, "Get the hell out. I'm calling the goddamn law!"

Reverend Leon kicked her in the head and ran.

She lay on the floor holding her head until her father's groaning roused her. She went to the bed. Daddy gazed at her. Red-black blood ran from his sores. Spit and tears ran down together on his chin and neck. Man was crying in the living room. Martha brought water and cleaned Daddy and changed the bed. She put an invalid feeder to his mouth and gave him lukewarm tea to drink.

His window turned into the indigo-tinted mirror in Mozelle's old apartment on the Place du Tertre in Montmartre. Mozelle sat in front of the mirror drinking vodka from a crystal glass. A table separated them. A bowl of caviar rested on a bed of ice. There were lemon slices on cobalt plates and toast pared of the crusts.

He saw his reflection in the blue glass. He watched his lips move as he spoke. He begged her not to go out tonight. He only had two more days in Paris. She slept all day in her apartment, then spent each night out in the company of an Egyptian cotton king, the latest in a succession of men to submit to her wild glamour.

"But the night is wonderful," she said, leaning, and rose to cool his forehead with a kiss. She removed her sable coat from the back of her chair. She had on black lace stockings beneath a red silk dinner dress. "I promise to be back by midnight. We can stay at home if you wish. We can be alone and talk. I promise."

Martha fell heavily into one of her vinyl kitchen chairs. She cursed and turned on the portable TV on the table. Diana Ross was on *The Muppet Show*. The telephone rang. It was Silk.

"What you want, nigger?" she raged into the phone.

"That's how you answer your phone, woman?"

"Don't give me word for word. Look, Mr. Ralston Edwards—"

"Chill out. I just called to see how you doing. How's my son?" He sounded high. She heard John Coltrane's "Naima" in the background.

"You aint got no son. Long as it took you to call to see is he living or dead."

"Baby, I—"

She had already hung up. She told herself she wasn't thinking about Silk. "Damn," she cursed aloud. She must have been crazy leaving that maniac alone in the room with Daddy like that. And getting burned for her whole welfare check! She needed help. She picked up the phone and dialed Peanut's number at the

Playbar, before she realized Peanut had taken the night off and was probably in Brooklyn by now. Peanut would not help her. What could Peanut do anyway?

Martha dialed information and got the Andersons' number across the street. When Daddy closed his churches he had forbidden his followers from coming near him. In all these years none of them had disobeyed his order. Even the Andersons had stayed away, though Martha often caught Sister Sarah staring at number 28 from her porch, looking across the brick-covered street as though the street were a river full of angry crocodiles. Would she come now?

Daddy had loved Sister Anderson. Sister Anderson and her boy were the only ones from the last days of his church whom Daddy had spoken about when he was well. He said he had taught her things—and her boy. He said Sister Anderson could perform the ritual for raising a dead man from the grave.

Would she come?

She still asked Martha about Daddy. Sarah had always used her to maintain some touch with Daddy, even though Martha looked like the kind of common negro Sarah detested. In the early times of Martha's imagination and memory, when Martha was six or seven, learning to roam the streets, Sister Sarah would encourage her to approach her house, luring her to the porch with cookies, egg salad sandwiches with the crust sliced off and pink lemonade. She was never admitted into the house. Her visits were at night. Sister Sarah would look at her with wide irises, as if she were able to forgive Martha for her raggedy dresses and her piss-smelling underpants. She could forgive the child's jungled hair, long before Martha began the treatments at Honey's, religiously having the lye applied which had transformed that bushy head. Into Sarah's mysterious and refined presence Martha would walk, coming like a pitcher before a fountain.

Sarah Anderson's face was so finely made that in profile it

resembled an antique coin. She would be dressed in some faded Parisian afternoon gown bordered with molded lace. On the dimly lit porch the old garment became her robe of state. Martha would watch her cooled ritualizing gestures, listening to the woman's strange talk explode in the air. Sister Sarah wore gold hoops in her ears that made a small, fascinating sound when she moved. She talked to Martha the way adults normally talk to children and animals. Sarah's voice laid siege to her until, finally, the long-necked nod and "You better go on home now." Martha rose and went down to meet the summer night at the curb—not knowing whether home tonight was in the apartment across the street or, if Daddy had a woman up there, beneath the back of 28, or if Peanut would find her and take her to her place on Quitman Street.

She had come to the porch one night, after playing stickball with a gang of boys on Stratford Place, holding together the ripped hem of her dress. Sister Sarah appeared suddenly and said, "Get down." Sarah had always spoken to her from her high porch after that. From then on Martha, woman and girl, received Sarah's gifts of food, money and kind words from the street. She never told anyone that once she had been suffered so close to the strange house of mirrors and crystal light fixtures—not even Peanut—fearing she might be called a liar and then be forced to doubt her visits on the deep porch herself.

Still, she kept Sarah's words inside her like a sacrament. She had barely been old enough to understand the woman's ceaseless talk, but she had *entered* the world with enough wisdom to feel and record its force.

"Your father was the life of all his followers. They worshiped him. Never let anyone poison you against him. He was a man, and there is good and evil in all men, but Daddy had something else. It was the strong selfish God in him. Daddy Poole was as great a man as they send the children to school to learn about.

Greater than that to you, child, because he had his miracle right here in these streets.

"His works laid the foundation. His preaching work here, his helping to bring the minerals and gemstones out of the earth in Africa, laid the foundation for the coming of the Son of Man. Everything he did laid the foundation for Christ to return in earth, even in Newark, just like he said. Daddy didn't do anything wrong in putting women in the world where they could be seen. That's only nature. It's the nature of flesh that it wants to be seen.

"People were always looking for Daddy's sin, but they don't know what sin is. God didn't flood the world because of sin. He didn't throw fire on Gomorrah because of sin. God knows how to deal with sin. It was people's stone-hearted condition, their preoccupation with ease, their self-centeredness in believing they *were* flesh that made God shut the doors of mercy and bring Hell to earth. Because they could not be penetrated. Because their souls could no longer tremble. That's what makes God destroy the world.

"It's people's stone-hearted attitude that has your father locked up in his house, hidden from the world, that has sorrow eating this city's heart. Daddy has poured out his wrath on Newark like water. But I still believe out of these ashes redemption will come. It's going to take some time, and I may not live to see it.

"You *have* to be broken, child.

"You must have a broken spirit before God. There is a precious annointing oil. Man will never smell the fragrance of that oil unless the vessel is broken. It is the annointing that breaks the yoke in people's lives. We *must* be broken. Our hearts must be penetrated.

"*Daddy broke us.*

"I believe we are living in the end time. Every day I'm living to live again. Just like in the days of Noah. Just like in the days of Sodom and Gomorrah, people refuse to be broken.

"In your father's church they did a dance when they received the power. The people would jerk and tremble. They leaped against the walls and rolled along the floor. They hollered and retched and some fell out in a dead faint. It was a whirling, sanctifying dance, and after that dance they walked with God in conversion, married to the Holy Ghost." She waved a hand at Prince Street. "The people need to dance that dance again.

"They let the times make them leave off following your father. Just like in the days of Noah, they hear the hammer ring and their hearts don't tremble. They see the ark and it doesn't affect them. They touch it, but there is no burning in their souls. *That* is the spirit of the end time, child.

"The world is going to reel. God is going to throw fire at the earth. It's going to be too late. The doors of mercy will be shut. Those that breathe will breathe in sulphur and flame. Hold on to your father. Let your heart and your mind be in the same place, and you will understand him. Ask God to break every power over you that separates you from him. He will bring your flesh into subjection in His own time."

Martha lit a Kool. She counted up her chances and dialed the phone.

Sister Sarah had come out to her porch hoping for a breeze. She caught up her streaming hair at the back of her neck, wishing a soft coolness would touch her there. It did not. She let her hair fall and sank into her chair. She fanned herself stirring no air. She sweated. The sun had gone out two hours ago. It was still as hot as noon. "I'm burning up," she told herself. "I'm just going to burn into a pyramid of ashes." She dragged her chair to the front of the porch and looked across at Daddy's house. Cars thundered back and forth in the middle of the street. The air was filled with the sound of Friday night. Music blared from boom-boxes. Windows were thrown high. Her neighbors were in front of their houses, with bare arms, their head rags removed, laughing and talking, leaning on cars. She smelled marijuana through the screen.

Daddy's house had a hard, chitinous look tonight. It was lit with the ghost light of the dead day. The windows at the front of the house were boarded. At the first story, beside the high, framed door, was a sign which read: HATS CLEANED & BLOCKED—SHOESHINE. The house on the left of Daddy's had been torn down, leaving a narrow, overgrown lot. The lot was strewn with garbage. The broken glass there glittered all day.

She thought she heard the phone ring and turned.

It occurred to her that she had become the sexless priestess Daddy had wanted, watching his house day in and day out, exiled in her own house of mirrors and crystal lamps. She felt her throat tighten. Jimmy Anderson would be along soon wearing his overalls and truck driver's cap, his pretty hair slipping over his forehead like rich black oil. He would smell of gasoline, sweat, cigarettes and Jade East cologne. He would barely greet her, then go to the back of the house and eat his dinner alone while she remained on the porch gazing at 28. He would move on to the bathroom upstairs where she had laid out fresh towels, his soaps and shaving items. She would get up and go in the kitchen to wash the dishes. The radio would be on in the living room. She would hear the water running upstairs. It would sound like the sad rain on a rainy day. Jimmy would stand before the mirror and carefully shave his face for an eternity while the water flowed from the spigots. He would humble himself on the toilet forever. Then in the porcelain tub filled with hot water and Chinese Wash he would bathe his yellow body again and again. He would rinse bergamot soap through his shiny spins of hair.

Sometimes he would sing to himself. Sometimes Jimmy Anderson would sing, and to Sister Sarah it would sound, at first, like moaning. This was the part of his homecoming that remained somehow, despite all repetition, new. At first utterance, wherever she happened to be in the house, his voice would stun her. She became arrested in whatever reverie she was involved at that moment. She would stop as one stops at the hearing of a warning bell. He had a beautiful voice. Sarah rarely understood the words and yet his songs flooded her mind with pictures. There was one particular song he often sang. Sarah had become familiar with it. She had learned the story of that particular song. It was an old gospel she knew as a child. When Jimmy Anderson sang this song, his voice seemed to travel through the house seeking her out. *In the sea.*

In the sea,

His voice would toll. Suddenly, the house no longer had walls or ceilings. The night and stars and mysteries entered.

In the sea,

The sound was so sad and lonely. It was the voice of a stranger. Jimmy Anderson was a stranger.

Somebody got drowned in the sea.

Somebody? Who got drowned? Who went into the sea? Who got drowned? The stranger. Got drowned. In the sea.

Moisture slid between her breasts. How had she remained married for thirty-seven years? She still felt young enough for her marriage to have been someone else's. Jimmy Anderson had not flaunted his adultery since that woman he used to keep on Court Street before the girls were born. Sister Sarah did not know who was loving her husband now. It was not she. Sarah had not worked and strained with her legs raised around him for more than six years. She had lost all taste for sex. She did not want her body explored by anyone again.

Turned around in her chair, looking into her own house, Sarah saw the scene it had taken her mind the whole summer to reach by a long-drawn chain.

She watched the vision pour from the backwaters of love-memory and time.

Her son was only a few months old. Emmett lay in the blue-if-it's-a-boy basinet in the living room, crying. A table and lamp were overturned near the basinet.

The snow outside whirled and spun past the windows.

She stood by the mantel stiff as a guard, furious words tumbling from her throat.

Jimmy Anderson sat on the sofa, his head leaning back, paying her no mind apparently.

They had been in the house all day arguing.

"If you don't like what you have here, then go on around to Court Street and live with your whore. And don't think you're coming back in here when she gives you the clap."

His head came forward slowly. He stood and walked past her and the basinet and stood at the window. The snow whispered against the house. She wanted to ask him if he could hear it too just beneath Emmett's cries. Finally he said in a flat, hoarse voice, looking off at the dark, empty street, "Watch what you say about Alice. She aint got nothing to do with this. Alice is a good woman. She may not have your light skin and straight hair, but she's decent. If she'd had a baby, I'll tell you one damn thing, I'd *know* it was mine."

She went after him with her hands on her hips, her low-heeled shoes slurring against the floor.

"Then go on to your disease-breeding bitch," she told the back of his head.

"I told you one time to watch yourself, woman." Danger and warning rode his voice.

"And I told you Emmett is not Sam Poole's baby. I don't have to lie. Why you wait till now to start bringing this shit up? I say go on to your Court Street whore then. You don't do a thing for me I can't get somebody else to do."

He came around and struck her on the side of her face. "Don't talk to me like that."

Sarah did not flinch. He struck her a second time. She reached out and gripped the back of his ears with her nails. She brought him stumbling forward. They struggled and hit each other. Sarah's right breast worked its way free of her housedress. Jimmy slammed her against the basinet. She flung out her arms to break her fall.

"All right, woman. This what you want, huh?" He said it again: "This what you want." He twisted her arm behind her back. Her wild hair brushed Emmett's face. "You *like* to have your ass kicked."

She stepped out of her shoes. When he slacked the pressure on her arm she hurled around and started hammering his cock through his pants. "You nasty motherfucker," she shouted. "I'll kill you. I'll kill you." She punished the front of his pants until he backed away from her. He tried to snatch her shoe from her, but Sarah struck his hands. She swung the heel across his neck and he dropped to one knee.

"Shit," he moaned.

She came by him. He pulled her to the floor on her face. He jumped on her back, pounding her head against the floor.

Jimmy looked up suddenly and saw Daddy come into the house through the vestibule as if moving in the very breath of life. Daddy was carrying an automatic gun.

Jimmy slammed Sarah's face to the floor. "Man, get the fuck out of my house!"

Daddy had owned a copy of the key to number 27 for nine years. He was standing just outside the living room by the newel. He walked into the room, the gun's muzzle sighting down on Jimmy's head. His mouth held a smile that barely stretched his lips.

"If you don't get up off her, I'll blow your craven ass out of the world this same minute, boy."

Jimmy rolled over, Sarah got up and went to the mantel to check herself in the mirror. She fixed her dress. Her hair looked like a wild, tropical plant. A purplish bruise ran along one side of her face. In the mirror she saw Daddy open his jacket and place his gun in his belt. She watched his jeweled hand work quickly at the button again, fastening the jacket.

The baby had stopped yelling. The snow murmured into the house's frame.

All at once she felt her face smarting, the blood throbbing in her head.

"Get off the damn floor," Daddy said to Jimmy. "When you going to start acting like a man in this house, or you just going to be a boy your whole life?"

"I *am* the man in this house, and what goes on in here is my business."

"How it's your business and you going to fight your woman in front of the window with the blinds up?"

He sat Jimmy on the sofa pointing his finger in Jimmy's face. "Let me tell you one goddamn thing, boy. If you ever hit that woman again, I'll have your balls. Are you with that? I can have your death a hundred ways, Jimmy, but I swear I'll kill you myself. Now you just try me. When I brought Sarah back to Newark and gave her to you again it wasn't a light thing. That's the *last* wife you going to have in this world, and you're her last husband. You better *act* like you have good sense, if you don't.

"All right then," Daddy turned with a weary look. "Turn on that TV set and let your man watch television in his own house in peace, then get this place cleaned up."

Sarah walked over to the cabinet and turned on the television. She went to the sideboard and poured two shots of gin and brought them to Jimmy and Daddy. Then she began setting the room in order.

Daddy downed his drink. He lifted Emmett from the basinet. He sat and wiped away Emmett's tears. He called for a diaper, wiped the baby's ass and changed him. He loosened his wide, pearl-gray necktie, a proud, harsh-loving god, holding the baby in a corner until the hour was late.

When he got up to leave he brought Emmett over to her. She was sitting on the sofa next to Jimmy. Jimmy had fallen asleep. He placed the baby gently in her lap.

"This is still what you want?"

She told him yes.

"Then take good care of it."

His hand brushed her breasts and stroked her neck. In that gesture and moment she felt him escape into her. That was the last time he had touched her. Daddy was the butter that made the rest of her life easy to swallow. Now, on her dark porch, Sarah began to weep. Her body sent up a moan, from love-hunger and deep wounds, tearing and healing her. Then she heard her phone ringing.

Daddy was awake. He said no when she asked him if he was in pain, but Martha could see his body stiffen and shudder. She sat him up in the bed and combed his hair.

"Babygir'?"

"Yeah?"

"Wind up the clock on the night table, baby."

"I will."

"What time is it?"

"Quarter to eleven."

"Where is she?" He meant Mozelle.

"She say she'll be here." She meant Sister Sarah.

"There she goes," said Iphigenia, standing by the window in her mother's room. Patti came up behind her. They watched Sarah Anderson cross Prince Street. "She's going over there."

"I hope she stay over there," Patti said. "I hope he get her over there and kill her. I'm sick of her." Patti clapped her hands and chanted:

> *Little Sally Walker sitting in a saucer*
> *Waiting for the old man to bring her a dollar*
> *Rise, Sally, Rise*
> *Put your hand on your hip*
> *Let your backbone slip*
> *Ah, shake it to the east*
> *Ah, shake it to the west*
> *Shake it to the very one that you love the best*

Sister Sarah rang the bell. It was more than sixteen years since she last stood at his door. Up close she saw how badly the house needed repairs. The short limestone steps were eroding. The paint on the door was cracked and peeling. Nicknames and obscenities had been carved in the boards covering the store window.

Martha came down with Man in her arms. Sister Sarah wiped her feet at the door and walked in slowly where there were once brocaded walls and a bright Persian carpet. Now it was only a blackened hallway where junkies broke in during the winter and used the place for a shooting gallery.

She tried to check her revulsion in his room when she saw how time had worked away at Daddy. His exquisite face was now rawboned, like a face dug from the ground. She smelled his stench the moment she entered.

Martha went into the kitchen.

Sarah felt panic. His hands and feet twitched anxiously when he caught sight of her in the room. His hands looked like feet. She did not want to go near him.

He was setting his mouth to say something. He was a long time forming the words.

"What is truth?" he asked.

She approached the bed with tears in her eyes. He had received her with the greeting of the voodoo priestess by the *hungan*-priest. Daddy took her to Haiti in 1953. He took her over the island—Port-au-Prince, Jacmel, Artibonite Valley—showing her the customs and the rites. They worshiped at the famous shrines. She knew the greeting.

"What is truth?"

Sister Sarah lifted her dress and showed him her vagina. "Here is truth." She stepped back, sat in the straight-backed chair and held his hat and cane.

When Jimmy got home from the swing shift, all the lights were on inside his house. The front door was unlocked. He found his daughters standing as still as idols in their mother's bedroom with the key in the door, raptly listening to a Bud Powell record. Face powder was spilled on the dressing table and floor. The room overflowed with discarded gowns, hats and feathers.

"What the hell is going on in here? Where is your mother?"

Iphigenia cut her eyes at him. "She went to Twenty-eight," she said through her bucked teeth.

Jimmy felt blocked in the middle of his body. "She went to Daddy Poole's house?"

"Yes," Iphigenia said, "about an hour ago."

He felt himself burst headlong into some unknown region. *At Daddy's house?* He was more troubled than surprised. He turned and ran down the steps. In his front door he hung back. Daddy Poole was dying. The knowledge came to him in the hot night air. He looked across the street and saw the sharp silhouette of Savannah Sparks sitting in the back of a yellow cab parked in front of 28. Her head was inclined toward the house.

Jimmy touched death in the air. He saw Death standing in the ravaged street. The annointing of Daddy's life and death was on everything. The same annointing that had made Daddy's name in Newark and brought deliverance to a captive people, made saints of thieves and prostitutes, healed the sick—was upon him now. It was in Jimmy's bones and in his clothes. With that annointing returned the hope of an impossible reconciliation of spirit and flesh. He testified to the night: "I thank God for Sam Poole." He had not known anything more stalwart in his life than the love of Sam Poole. He had been there. He had seen the miracles. He had prayed and wept at the altar down at the Broome Street church. He received the baptism of the Holy Spirit the same night his wife did. Jimmy had done everything Daddy told him. He slept in a coffin for nine days until all his enemies were dead. He wore his hat backward until hard luck got off his trail. He did everything Daddy told him until Daddy's spirit became his breathing and moving. He fasted. He prayed. He received the word of God. He went down in the water and came up dancing under the high arm of God. Daddy had chosen him to do his will. He filled Jimmy with a spark of his own fire, and just a spark of that fire had kept Jimmy burning down through the years, through wars, work, women and babies—in Daddy's presence and in his mystical absence. He had chosen Sarah, but Daddy had chosen him. It was the mystery of that choosing that had Jimmy Anderson stopped in the frame of his door, bound by a weave of thoughts.

Sister Sarah sat praying beside Daddy's bed. Man began to cry in the front room. His cries pierced into her mind. She looked up when Martha came in carrying Man with a pacifier in his mouth.

Sarah backed away from the bed, knocking over the straight-backed chair. Daddy was mightily pulling himself up, laughing without real laughter in his voice. Something was in the room—something that was not there before. Daddy pulled back the covers and placed his feet down at the side of the bed. His feet moved around, feeling for his slippers.

He reached out to hold the bedpost to stand up. With his arm outstretched, a vivid pain stabbed him, and he began to die. Sarah saw the stroke twist the side of his face. He fell and doubled over on the floor.

Martha screamed. She ran to the bed, stepping over her father, and tore the snakehide from the wall. Sarah came and took Man from her, cajoling in a whisper, "Lord, child."

"Motherfucker," Martha screamed. "No!" She took the snakehide into the kitchen and set fire to it in the sink. It crackled and burned up in a moment. "No, motherfucker!" She screamed, fleeing the house.

She did not stop until she was in front of Mr. Wonderful's Bar and Lounge. She pushed past the flashy players standing on the sidewalk. There was no one on the door. So many hustles went on inside the club, the management did not need to rely on a cover charge to keep turning a profit.

The club was crowded with people Martha had seen her whole life, "homegirls" and "bloods" dressed in their best clothes, posing and moving with sweaty grace in the carnival-colored air. Martha was still wearing her maid uniform. *Just as I am, Lord/without one plea/but that your blood was shed for me. . . .* The old hymn went through Martha's mind as she entered the nightclub. The words did not remind her of Jesus or even Daddy, but of the blood-stained woman named Blanche whom Peanut said had been her mother. *Just as I am, Lord,* pouring out of the chocolate, lemon and cherry women's faces she saw around her—women, sisters, strangers painted and pushed into tight dresses and perched on treacherously high shoes, lined up like decoys for other women who had faded from Newark. The long, smoky room swung in and out of time. How could Martha ever know if the things Peanut had said were true? All Martha could do was know what happened to her in her own time.

The music in the place splintered Martha's thoughts.

There was a dance floor in the center of the room with tables surrounding it on three sides. The stage was at the head of the dance floor. Silk stood on the stage, fronting an eight-piece band. He wore a white tuxedo and white bucks. His hair was a glazed ridge of curls, crusted with grease and lye.

The band played a slow blues. The baritone sax anchored Silk's alto sax. The song took on a rough majesty under the flourishes of the doubled saxophones.

Silk stepped into a lavender spotlight and muscled a tight solo, relaying the song's colorful figures with dreamy twists and turns. The ceiling and walls were painted black and stenciled with silver stars. The music exploded inside Martha. She opened herself to the music, her arms dangling, her gross mouth slack.

The piano and drums reentered suddenly, pushing the song into an oiled, over-the-top timing. The brass voices wailed over the knocked-out rhythm. The music weaved through blues, gospel, ragtime, jazz and funk.

Martha's truncated amazon's body became fused. Her mind snapped free. She clapped her hands, straining against the fabric of her maid uniform. Martha moved her hips, fucking the bitter night.

She began to dance. The music piled up crescendo after crescendo. Her body quickened and jerked. She twisted and snaked out in the center of the dance floor, performing small, dervish spins and body-popping turns. She lifted her arms, stretching her hands, and shook the way the dark sisters shook in Newark's Pentecostal churches, thrusting her shoulders, leaning into the music with endlessly rocking hips. She flung back her head and shook herself free and clear.

She could no longer see the room before her. She lost the rhythm of the music. Martha fainted. She saw her father resting on a throne chair in a white pavilion, coming down from God. His eyelids trembling, his eyes turned inward, he ripped from his chest the moving, bleeding heart. When she came to, she was sitting at a table by the door. Two women were fanning her with perfumed handkerchiefs. At first she thought the hand-kerchiefs were birds flying up from her body.

Martha stood. Well-muscled men and women with long backs were leaping on the dance floor. Martha felt hot and good. She felt clean. She turned from the place and moved with a strange aspect she had not recognized in herself before.

She went outside and walked back to Prince Street under her father's shadow.